Silent Wings

Jo Hammers

Paranormal Crossroads & Publishing

Table of Contents

1. A Peeping Tom's Confession   7

2. Love at First Peep   24

3. The Teacher's Lounge   39

4. Two Peeping Toms   52

5. Questionable Creme and Dentures   61

6. Prom Time for Jodi   68

7. Arrest of the Judge   83

8. Jackie's Prom   90

9. Wedding Bells   105

10. Surprise Visitor   118

11. The Obituary Carmen   130

12. The High Flyer   142

13. Life Takes a New Direction   160

Silent Wings

Jo Hammers

CHAPTER ONE

A PEEPING TOM'S CONFESSION

I am a window peeper. It is an acquired addiction. I am harmless other than I am nosy and want to see what people do behind closed doors and closed curtains. I would not hit another human or abuse them in any way physically. I just like to peep in thru windows and see what they are up to. My mother always said I was curious as a cat. It is more that curiosity. I get a high, a thrill, a sense of who I am from peeping. As a young teenager, I looked thru windows to sense what families were like. My family was comprised of alcoholics and drug addicts. I fantasized about having parents who saw me thru sober eyes and spoiled me with love. The following is my take on three years in my life when I was seeking what I did not have thru window peeping. Since then, I have channeled my curiosity and talent for peeping into a structured, legal vocation.

It was New Year's Eve and I was in my sophomore year of high school. My family was composed of the city's lowest forms of alcoholics and drug addicts. We were the scum of the city and lived across the tracks as they say. We lived in the poorest end of town and in the worse paint peeled house on my block. There were plans at my house for New Year's Eve, but it wasn't what most humans did celebrating the night. When New Year's Eve masses were drinking and keeping the cops busy, my parents would begin to cook a new batch of meth.

My maternal grandmother and older sister, who lived with us in our tiny two bedroom shack with the front door falling off, were well on their way to tying on a New Year's Eve alcoholic stupor. My sister, who was ten years older than me, had been an airline stewardess. She moved back home on Christmas Eve encroaching on my bedroom which was a lean-to back porch. She had been fired from her airline for drinking on the job. I resented her moving back home. She escaped our family's addictions, was making good money, and had a great apartment. She threw it all away because she wouldn't stay out of a vodka bottle. Pilots and important business men dated her and bought her nice things. She was a drunk who threw it all away. She had her chance and was now worthless in my book. Someday, when I managed to abandon our roots, I was not looking back or throwing a good life away for a wine bottle or a fix. My sister's wings were silent and she was the one that killed them. I didn't feel sorry for her.

The only New Year's celebration I would be participating in would be the one I created peeping thru windows. My sister, who was ten years older than me, sat at the rickety kitchen table with her head down resting on one arm on the table. I glanced at my seventy year old grandmother who was sitting at the table with my sister. She was drinking and shooting up. She was a pathetic old hag that I wasn't particularly fond of. She was at the getting high, mouthy stage and I had no intentions of sticking around and listening to her rant on and on about some dude who had dumped her when she was my age. Equally annoying was when my sister in a drunken stupor would tell for the thousandth time about the pilot that threw her out over an empty bottle of wine. I wandered back to the lean-to porch that was my bedroom. I put on a black sweat shirt, black stocking hat, and gloves. When peeping, you had to blend in with the shadows of the night. My plan for the evening was to peep thru the back window of a huge house on Main Street. The house had a huge bouquet of black and white party balloons tied to its mailbox on the curb indicating a New Year's party was to be held there. Also, I had heard a woman talking about it with another woman as they were paying for gas at the down town convenience store. I always listened in on conversations. I was a fifteen year old fly on the wall with big ears and no friends

The monstrous Victorian house on Main Street was the biggest house on its block. Having huge windows, it was possible to stand outside without a ladder of any sort and peep in any of the first floor windows if the shades weren't drawn. I felt confident that the house would be lit up like a Christmas tree and the shades up to welcome arriving guests. There was bound to be lots of food and women with beautiful legs in high heels to peer at. I was a high-heel man then and I still am today. Feet and shoes stir the man in me. My sister, mother, and grandmother lay around drunk in the nude so much at home, that the female body held no mystery for me. I wasn't a boob man or a body man. The only thing I found sexy about a woman was her feet. I liked feet with painted toenails and wearing spikes. My mother, grandmother, and sister wore cheap discount store flip flops because they spent all their shoe money on booze.

I had walked past and looked the Main Street house over ahead of time. That was a skill I had learned early. You didn't want to waste several miles of walking in the cold after dark to find that windows were too high to peep thru. My choice of window was always the bathroom or kitchen one in the rear. Party or house guests arriving or leaving would not be flashing their car lights on you. Thru rear windows, I could pretty well peep as long as I wanted.

After putting on my ragged coat, I peeped into the kitchen to see if any of my family was interested in the fact that I was leaving. They weren't. Dad had already taken the meth ingredients to his paint peeled shed in the back that he called a garage. My mother had taken a seat at the front window with a full open bottle of wine in one hand. She would drink the whole damn thing. I knew her. My grandmother had fallen out of her kitchen chair and was lying on the dirty kitchen linoleum higher than a kite. My sister was passed out on the table. Her bottle of vodka was turned over and running out onto the floor. My family was pathetic drunks and I hated them. I wanted a real family to spend holidays with who made cookies and cheese balls. I didn't touch alcohol or drugs. I had made up my mind as a tiny child that I would not be a part of their drunken lifestyle when I was grown and got my chance to escape like my sister had.

Being the drug maker's kid made you the scum of the city, whether you were or not. You didn't get invited to parties or to homes to hang out. People feared you would return and clean them out, taking all of their valuables. I didn't have a girlfriend or a male friend to celebrate New Year's Eve with. I had become anti-social by choice. I was ashamed to take anyone decent to my house. I didn't see any point to it. They would dump me as a friend as soon as they saw where and how I lived.

My home was a shack that the plate below the walls was giving away and in places you could see the siding break-ing as well as the two by four studs beneath rotting off their plate. The windows had been hit so many times with thrown chairs and beer bottles that the glass was held in every window with multiple pieces of duck tape to keep out the weather. The front door was missing one hinge and only had a knob on the inside. The outside knob was missing and a piece of duck tape covered the hole. The front porch was missing one of its three posts and one end of the overhead was hanging down and expected to fall at any time. Down the driveway, at the rear of the house, was an old shed with all the paint peeled off it and overgrown with Poison Ivy vines. My father cooked meth there. No one wanted to fight the vines or the strewn path of bro-ken beer and liquor bottles to look in and see what he did back there. The driveway to the back was strewn with old car parts and discarded beer cans. The yard looked like a garbage dump and my parents wanted it that way. People stayed away. The back porch of the house was my bed-room till my sister came back forcing me to take the couch which only had two cushions instead of three. The inside of the house was alive with roaches and cabinets full of the poop from mice. If it came to a choice between bug spray and a bottle, the bottle always won out. There was never food in the house. I was lucky sometimes to find a cheap box of macaroni. My family did not eat, they drank. There was no stove or refrigerator in the kitchen. They had been sold long ago for money to make drugs. I had two sets of clothes and guarded them. My parents weren't past throw-ing up a garage sale sign and selling off any item of clothing given to any of us by charity. Nothing survived in our house to make it a home. If there was some small item that was important to me, I kept it safe in my locker at school. That included my school books and what little money I earned in the kitchen of the high school washing dishes at lunch one hour a day. I made about thirty dollars a week and I had to feed myself as well as buy my clothes out of it. Hanging out with friends and blowing a twenty was not an option. Most of the time I ate one meal a day and that was lunch at school. The school let me work it out taking out cafeteria trash when the school lunch hour was over.

So, lonely as hell, I left my family to their liquor and drugs. I headed out to ring in the New Year by peeping at the good lives of others. I was fifteen and fascinated with looking at platters of chocolate brownies, punch bowls of strange concoctions, and the pretty hi-heeled feet of respectable ladies. Later, I would have to find somewhere to sleep for the night. I was sure that one of the four drunks in my house or someone my parents sold a hit to would be crashed on my bed.

That New Year's Eve, I was just a fifteen year old kid who hadn't learned to fly yet. I was at the mercy of the wing clippers in my home. I dreamed of a respectable life with gorgeous, decent women as my companions and all the food I could eat. I hadn't reached the point where I was mature enough to turn my drunken family loose and fly away. Fate was going to have to let me fall out of the nest and hope that the world below would not eat me alive like a stray cat.

At fifteen, you are trying to figure out who the hell you are. One thing I was sure of, I was a foot man. When window peeping, I always looked at the women's feet first and then their faces. Not looking at their faces first, I decided that it was possible for me to love an older woman. Their feet when in spikes, did it for me just like those of the teens or college age girls. Some older women took good care of their feet. So, at fifteen I decided it was not necessary for me to settle on a girl my age. An old broad of thirty would be fine if she wore spikes and kept her toenails painted. So, at fifteen, I classified myself as a foot man who would never drink, do drugs, smoke, or live like my parents once I was grown. Other than that, I was trying to grow up and find myself. Looking in windows and dreaming was like television to me. I looked and idolized those I peeped at.

In childhood, I peeped at toys, dogs, and cats left on porches. As a young teen, I became a theme peeper. My nights of looking in windows were sort of like scavenger hunts. I would choose six items and peep thru different house windows till I found what was on my list for the evening. Sometimes I accomplished my hunt's goal in a couple of hours. Sometimes, it took all night. The hardest item I ever put on my scavenger peeping list was one of those hand held, women's, oriental fans. I looked in at least seventy five houses before I spotted anything that even half way resembled one. I finally settled for one of those fans they hand out in the summer at graveside funerals. It had a picture of Jesus on it and I decided that was about as oriental and exotic as I was going to find. I spent almost a week of nights looking for that illusive hand held, oriental woman's fan. A Chinese restaurant would have had them plastered all over the walls if I had peeped there. I was a fifteen year old dumb ass and I laugh at myself looking back.

On my desk today is a pencil cup. None of my clients

notice a folded up antique oriental fan stuck down in it. I bought it when I went in to business. It reminds me on a daily basis not to be a dumb ass. Also in the cup is an ink pen from the last air line my sister worked for. It is a reminder not to screw up my life as she did. My most treasured item in the cup is one red high heel broken off of a lady's shoe. It is a reminder for me to never quit looking for the woman who once wore it. She was the love of my life at fifteen. She disappeared leaving no trace of what might have happened to her. All I have of her is that single red spike and a small photo.

On that New Year's Eve, I made my way to the house on Main Street and walked around to the rear of the house in the shadows. There were too many people in the kitchen doing their thing for me to peep there. I was afraid they might come spilling out the back door and catch me on the porch. Instead, I chose to start my peeping at the rear bathroom window.

People are notorious for cracking their bathroom window to hide smells or let shower steam escape. I knew a kid at school who was a peeper and a sniffer. He got off on sniffing the bottles of shampoo and body soaps that sat perched on open window sills. Had I ever found a pair of gorgeous feet with painted toenails wearing spikes on an open bathroom window sill, I might have become a peeper and a sniffer. I like the smell of toe nail polish. However, I have never had the privilege of finding a pair of hi-heeled feet resting on a bathroom window sill and I have no interest in smelly shampoos.

I was not going to have any trouble peeping in the Main Street House bathroom. An outside, square air conditioning unit sat just below the bathroom window. I climbed up on it ducking beneath the window ledge and then rising slowly to peep in so as not to frighten anyone. The room was empty. I glanced at a framed poster on the wall opposite the lavatory of a female trapeze artist. That was cool! I examined the silk looking little rope climbing shoes she had on with ribbons winding up her legs. They were not spikes, but I liked them. Her feet were definitely a number nine on my one to ten feet scale. I wondered what her name was. For a moment, I imagined her flying thru the air and some athletic dude catching her.

There were at least fifteen cars parked out in the front in the drive and along the curb. With a crowd that size, it wouldn't take long for someone to have to use the facilities. I was right. In about five minutes or so, an old gray headed grandmother type entered, sat on the stool and pulled a pack of cigarettes from her black pants suit pocket. She wasn't using the John, so I knew she was hiding out to smoke. She appeared to be talking to herself as she rose and started looking thru the medicine cabinet. I couldn't see her feet. The space was too small. I looked her over real good. I always wanted a respectable granny I could introduce my friends to. She had on a conservative little black pantsuit with a jacket that buttoned down the front. She had on little gold rimmed glasses and on her fingers were those old fashioned type rings, the ones with colored stones for kids or grandkids birth dates. She was definitely my idea of what a granny should look like. I wanted her for my own. I wished I could have seen her feet. The feet on my women had to be beautiful. I was a foot man. My granny could have a bunion pad on as long as her toenails were painted and she was wearing spikes. Standing at the window, I watched her go thru every drawer in the bathroom looking for who knows what. Then, I wondered if she was an inside version of me. She did not put any-thing into her pockets, but she quickly scanned everything over from toothpaste to medicine bottles. I got the biggest delight out of her examining what appeared to be a little pink case of birth control pills. I watched as she pulled her granny glasses down on her nose so she could read the lit-tle pink case's instructions and the pharmacy sticker on it.

It was at that point that I thought it might be fun to scare another peeper like me. She was a Peeping Tom, plus a handler of things. I thought it would be funny to just tap on the window, let my face show, scare her, and then run before anyone caught me. So, I eased up to the window and watched for a minute as she continued to read items in the medicine cabinet. When she glanced toward the window where I had my face pressed against the glass, I tapped. To my surprise, she didn't scream, flip the lights out, or exit the room in haste. Instead, she shuffled over to the bath tub, raised the window, and offered me a cigarette from her pack. I didn't move. She had my full attention.

"I won't tell on you, if you don't tell on me. Would you like a cigarette?" She asked politely.

I immediately turned the cigarette down shaking my head no. I had watched my mother and dad waste all the mon-ey in my house buying booze and cartons of cigarettes. I never had the things that I needed as a kid, yet they had their cigarettes and booze. I was always the worst dressed kid in the class and had none of the toys and other items normal kids had. My family was made up of self-centered smoking drunks.

"Why didn't you run or scream when I made faces at you? "I asked out of curiosity. I didn't know her and she didn't know me.

"I made that face hundreds of times when I was your age. You are going to have to work on your scare technique if you want to be a seasoned peeper like me? Did you see anything interesting as you watched me check out the medicine bottles and personal items?"

"I liked the way you pushed your gold rimmed glasses down on your nose when you read the bottles. The only other individual that I have ever seen do that is my welfare pediatrician. His glasses slip down on his nose when he writes prescriptions or stares down at me from his six foot frame. It is very intimidating. You won't tell any other peeper that I see a kid welfare doctor will you?"

"No, I won't tell. My name is Granny Snoop. What is yours? You can choose a name that only we of the trade will recognize you by."

"Call me Bump." I shot back thinking of my face full of pimples and then asked. "There are other peepers like you and me?"

"There are lots of us in the trade and we peep for many different reasons. What is yours?"

"I have this compulsion to count things before I go to sleep. I choose an item and I peep in windows till I see six of it. My nervousness leaves and I can sleep. I guess I am a theme peeper. Sometimes I count bathroom lights left on, how many houses have someone sleeping on the couch, or maybe how many leave their televisions on after midnight. I have to count six of something. It usually is not about the people in the houses."

"That is interesting. What item are you counting peeping thru bathroom windows tonight?"

"Empty toilet paper rolls." I replied. "You would be surprised how many people will use the last of the toilet paper and not replace the roll on the spindle."

The elderly lady glanced down by the stool at the paper spindle. Sure enough, it was empty and a spare roll of paper sat on the back of the stool where it had been opened and used but not put on the empty roller.

"That is a good one, Bump. How many have you counted tonight?"

"The count is two so far. I will get my quota by ten. There are a lot of parties going on and the rolls will fly off the rollers. What is your choice to handle and peep at?" I asked.

"Medicine bottles fascinate me. You can tell a lot about people by what they put in their bodies." She stated puffing away on her cigarette."

"That cigarette isn't good for your body." I stated grinning at her thru the window. "Do you drink too? My parents do both."

"We all have our quirks and bad habits. A good smoke is mine. I actually prefer cigars but my granddaughter would kill me if she caught me with one."

"I guess you are right about the habits. With me, it is soda and chocolate bars. My face says it all. Have you peeped at any good cure alls for acne in your medicine bottle peeping?"

"Time, washing your face regular, and watching the soda and candy is the only thing I know of. It is a hormone thing. You will grow out of it." She replied and then added. "Have you tried to give them away?"

"What do you mean?"

"Every night before you go to bed, after you have washed your face, ask the Great Pimple Man who made them to take them back and give them to someone else? He eventually will. It is sort of like receiving a present at Christmas that you absolutely hate. If you give it back to the person and tell them how much you hate it, they will not be very likely to ever give you that gift again. Make the Great Pimple Man mad enough and he isn't likely to gift you with another fine batch. It usually takes about three years to convince him."

I laughed. This old woman was my type of person. She was just humorous enough to make me crazy about her. My own mother and grandmother did nothing but yell and tell me how worthless and stupid I was. "You are okay in my book, Granny Snoop. It is my lucky night meeting you."

"You are okay in mine, too. It takes a peeper to understand a peeper."

"Have you met any really interesting peepers like you and me? " I asked.

"Sure! I once met a midget who carried a step ladder on his peeping adventures. We called him Ladder Man."

"What was his bag? What did he peep at?" I asked out of curiosity."It had to be a lot of trouble for a little fellow to carry a step ladder with him especially if he needed to run afterwards.

"He had an obsession with tall girls. He peeped because he was afraid to ask them out, being so short."

"That makes sense. What did you peep at when you were young like me?" I asked wanting to get to know her a little better.

"I peeped thru the key holes of the apartments in our building. I was a foster child and I guess I was looking for the perfect family. The family I lived with yelled at me and called me names. Beyond the key holes was who I wanted to be. Now, I like bathrooms and medicine cabinets. What thrills you?"She asked pulling the pack of cigarettes from her pocket once more, lighting a second one, and then once more offering me one. I refused again.

"The thrill is getting to sleep when I am done. I have a compulsion to count before I sleep. When I was little, I counted the items in our apartment. After awhile, the items grew boring to me and I needed something new to count to be able to sleep. I am hoping the counting will go away when I'm grown. My mother used to get drunk and yell at me when I was a little kid. She was always high and yelling by my bedtime. It started about the time I was learning to count. In my mind, I would count as far as I could which was to six. When I was concentrating on counting, I didn't hear her yelling or fighting with my dad. Counting became a sleeping pill to me. I can't sleep at night now unless I count something. Tonight, I am counting empty, off the roller, toilet paper rolls instead of staying home and listening to my mother and dad have at it. They are downing a bottle of Vodka as well as some drugs. I won't go home tonight. I will crash somewhere when I am thru, somewhere where it is safe. I know where there are several vacant houses."

"You and I have a lot in common, Bump. I am not going to be able to sleep till I know what my Granddaughter is up to. The birth control pills there are hers. I may need a sleeping pill."

"Why do you handle things, Granny Snoop? I never touch anything."

"I want my granddaughter to have a good life. I don't want her getting pregnant while she is in high school and ruining her life. I guess I am snooping tonight to save her stupid little ass."

"So you are snooping to protect someone you love?"

"I am snooping trying to figure out who she is sneaking out to see."

"So one of your children and your granddaughter lives here?"

"Something like that . . .," she replied and then quickly added. "I live in one of those old folks hi-rises."

"I promise you I won't peep here anymore now that I know it is your family. There is honor amongst fellow window peepers to consider." I replied trying to sound like a respectable peeper."

"I won't peep in your house either." She replied grinning. "Next weekend, I am attending a party at the Nelson's house two doors east. Why don't you drop by the back window at nine and we can swap peeping stories for the week. You and I both know we can't share peeping with just anyone, especially family."

"It is a deal. You wouldn't sneak me a napkin full of goodies from the kitchen party table would you? I have often wondered what the goodies taste like at gatherings like this. I never get to eat, I just peep?"

"I will sneak you a napkin of goodies and hand them out the back door to you and then you run. It is bad Karma for two peepers to be working the same house."

"I like chocolate, if there are any brownies. I never get anything like that at home."

"I will make you a whole pan of brownies and hand them out the back window to you at the Nelsons if you will do me a favor this week."

"What would that be?"

"Take one night off from peeping and as you lay in your bed ask the Great Smoke Man six times to take my habit from me. Your prayers repeated will give you the count to six for your night. Helping others sometimes helps us with our own problems." She replied reaching out the window and lightly patting my check with her elderly well manicured hand.

She didn't realize that her hand on my face was magic. No one had ever loved me or patted me. I will never forget the feeling of her touch. I wanted to cry. I was like a sponge who wanted more of her.

"It is a deal." I replied and then left my position at the bathroom window to wait for her by the house's back door. She handed out to me a paper plate loaded with things that I had never tasted and didn't have a clue what some of them were. There was cheese, chips, crackers, cookies, candy, nuts, etc. It was piled. I took it, kissed her on her cheek surprising her, and then ran till I spotted a child's plastic play house, crawled inside, and ate my treats in the dark.

Granny Snoop and I became great friends and met regularly with her telling me weekly where she would be and what time to meet her at which window. On Monday nights, I did not window peep. I prayed six times on that night for Granny Snoop to give up smoking and for the big bump man to take back his gift. I was fifteen. I believed what people told me.

Each week, Granny Snoop would tell me she had smoked one cigarette less and that made me feel good about the counting. Over the next few months, she became the grandmother I so desperately wanted. My own maternal grandmother drank, yelled, and cursed me. Granny Snoop listened to me for ten minutes at designated windows and encouraged me to be all that I could be for the next week at school. I scolded her each week and told her to try to give up two or three more cigarettes so my prayers could be answered. She always agreed and I always continued to ask the Big Smoke Man six times to help her give up the habit. Surprisingly, my pimples started clearing up. I began to feel I had an in with the Great Smoke Man and the Big Bump Man. I knew nothing about religion or God. Praying was new to me. Granny Snoop introduced me to prayer and to the Big Smoke Bump Man. Granny Snoop made a believer out of me. Some men say the Sabbath is on Saturday and others say it is Sunday. My Sabbath is Monday night.

CHAPTER TWO

LOVE AT FIRST PEEP

Blizzard months are hard for peepers for obvious and non-obvious reasons. For one, it is cold. People go inside and pull their curtains to keep out drafts. Secondly, your tracks in the snow can lead law enforcement right back to you, especially if you are a kid. The smart peeper goes to the mall in snowy weather and peeps legally thru storefront windows. I am a glutton for punishment and always have been. Snowy weather did not stop me.

It was a whiteout blizzard March night when I was braving the weather to satisfy my need to peep so I could sleep. The wind was blowing, howling, and causing deep snow drifts to form. The night was white and glistening with a new fallen snow. Braving the weather, I made my way to a residential section in the nicer part of the city where everyone thought they were safe from people like me. I was bundled up in dark clothing and not thinking too swift for a young peeper of fifteen. I should have been dressed in white.

I was a theme peeper and chose for that blizzard screaming night a scavenger hunt peep for six fans and they had to be in use. I was sure that I would not find any and that would allow me to stay out all night escaping having to go home. My parents had just made a batch of drugs and were selling it out the door of the back porch. It was not a safe moment to be at home, and I knew it. All the low life of the city would enter and leave making their drug buys. I liked to challenge myself in choosing something ordinary to look for, but at the same time hard to find in off seasons.

My first stop peeping in a window went smoothly. I watched an older man in his garage painting what looked like tire rims. He had a fan going for ventilation. I bored quickly with him. His garage reminded me too much of my dad's. My father cooked meth in the garage and kept a ventilation fan going. I counted the old fellow's box fan. It was number one for the evening.

Next, I peeped at a woman doing dishes who looked tired. As nice of a house as she had, I wondered why she didn't have a dishwasher. I always questioned what I saw. I decided hers was on the fritz and she was waiting for a plumber to get to her. The nicer houses always had service trucks in the driveways. Across the tracks where I lived, nothing ever got fixed. I did not see a fan of any sort, so I moved on.

Next, I found a side window on a small bungalow that didn't have the drapes drawn. I waded the twelve or so inches of snow and peeped in from the side. An old woman sat in a lounge chair with her feet up, curlers in her hair, green stuff on her face, and wearing the worst grandma clothes I had ever seen. Even worse, she wore white men's socks that had holes in the toes and heels. She would have scared any little kid to death if it had been Halloween. I would have hated to be the kid that rang her bell and then wet my pants seeing her in that get up. She definitely was not eye candy. The only thing happening inside that house was her flipping the TV remote. Glancing toward her ceiling, I did see that she had her overhead ceiling fan on circulating her living room heat. I had to count that as a fan. People did use them in the summer time. Her fan was number two, I moved on.

Up to that point, my evening of peeping had been pretty ordinary. The one thing I discovered in my years of peeping up to that point was that people didn't always look their best behind closed doors. You saw them like they really were. The movies showed beautiful women with peepers and murderers coming to call. What I found behind drawn window shades were people wearing their worse and looking their worse. Rarely did you see a great pair of legs or a beautiful girl in nightwear.

I started peeping at the age of eight. My parents never cared where I was and I longed for what the other kids on my street had. I wanted a family who ate at the table and a clean bed to sleep in. I just wandered about watching my neighbors thru doors and windows. Sometimes they caught me and fed me. Others yelled and told me to stay off of their property. Sometimes I would end up twelve or fifteen blocks from home and I was only in the second or third grade. It was a wonder some pervert hadn't snatched me up. I would have welcomed anyone who paid me the least bit of attention. I received absolutely none at home.

A few doors down from the old lady in curlers, I spotted a house with all the windows undraped. I peeped in the front window and saw a pretty girl sitting on a couch watching TV. She was nicely dressed like she had just returned home from an office job and hadn't bothered to put on her old clothes yet. I decided to circle around and peep from the back so that I couldn't be seen from the street. All the windows were undraped and the lights were all on. I was sure that there were other things going on in the house to take a look at.

Around in the back, I was delighted to find a tall snow dusted evergreen bush that I could hide behind. I peeped thru French doors into the kitchen and eating area. A jock of a man in his mid twenties was cooking. I watched as he flipped a couple of burgers in a pan on the stove and then laughed for some reason. I thought that seemed a little odd. Why would you laugh in the middle of flipping burgers? I continued to watch.

He continued to smile like a Cheshire cat. Then curling clouds of smoke started escaping from his stove. I snorted and broke out into a grin as I watched him pull a pan of burnt French fries from his oven and frantically blow them like his breath could put out the flames. He then grabbed a tea towel and was waving crazily with one free arm at a smoke alarm to get it to go off. Then he sat the hot pan of smoking black fries down on the stove top and quickly turned the exhaust on. I watched as the smoking pan's curls and swirls of smoke started heading toward it. I liked peeping on older dudes who weren't as in control as they thought they were. I was on a fifteen year old high watching him dance around with a tea towel trying to rid of the smoke. It was better than any reality comedy bit I had seen on TV.

I ducked behind the evergreen when he opened the doors to let fresh air in and throw the French fries out into the snow. Then I watched him in a frenzy digging in his kitchen cupboard looking for something. The man was in a panic. I grinned as he pulled down a half empty bag of potato chips of some sort and pull a quick handful from the bag and toss them haphazardly on the two plates. He had lost his cool and his Cheshire cat laugh. He was now winging it. I could see that he was panicked. It was moments like that I longed for. It was a real life funny situation that I could laugh about later.

I was considering moving on to another house, when I was appalled at something he did. After he poured two glasses of wine, he stirred a powdered substance into one of the glasses. I had participated in the say no to drugs program in health class at school. It had included a caution to girls to not leave their glasses unattended at parties. This dude looked like he was spiking one of the drinks. I questioned what I was seeing. Maybe that glass was his and he was putting some medicine for himself in it. I tried to give him the benefit of doubt. Then he almost caused me to throw up.

Granted it was winter and there were a lot of chest and head colds happening. However, most people were not into purposely sharing them. I watched as he hocked up from his lungs and throat a wad of flam which he proceeded to spit onto the top of the burger next to the glass of powdered wine. He then put the bun top on. Grossed out, I gagged and was outraged. There was a beautiful unsuspecting girl in his living room that he planned to take advantage of in a degrading way. I watched as he picked the tray up to head for the living area of the house. Suddenly, he set the tray down taking time out to answer a cell phone that lay on the counter.

I had to intervene. That girl could be my sister. Sprinting, I circled the house checking my shirt pocket for an ink pen as I went. Standing on the front entrance, I quickly pulled a scrap piece of notebook paper from my pocket that I carried to jot down thoughts on. At that point in my life, I thought I wanted to be a writer. I quickly scribbled a note:

Don't eat the food. The man in the kitchen hocked up, spit on your burger, and put a powder in your drink. You are in trouble. A friend

I hurriedly rang the door bell. If he answered, I would ask directions. Luckily, she came to the door. I was pleased taking a quick glance at her. She had on the cutest short black boots with high heels on them. She was his guest. If she lived there, she would have taken them off at the door wanting to relax.

"May I help you?" she asked looking me over. "Jake is busy in the kitchen.

I handed her the note and then ran like hell till I was blocks away from the area in case she called the police. I couldn't get caught window peeping. My mother would kill me. Skipping school or staying out all night was not a problem with her. Window Peeping was a different story. Her and my father tried to avoid any confrontation with the law. They cooked meth in the back shed to make a living and support their habits. Petty crime on my part would bring policemen calling. That would get me beat. I hated my family and definitely would never do the drug bit. I had signed the pledge to say no to drugs at school.

Out of breath and blocks away from the nicely dressed chic at the door, I leaned on the side of a trash dumpster. My rapid breathing was making a cloud form in front of me in the icy air. It was a beautiful night and the land-scape was white. I looked behind me and saw that my tracks were the only ones in the new fallen snow. I then realized that all the police had to do was follow my tracks to find me. Now what was I going to do? I couldn't let the tracks lead to my house.

Fifteen year olds don't always think too swift. Chances were, the girl after reading the note, left appreciating the warning. Calling the police and turning in a do-gooder peeping Tom was probably not on her priority list. The pervert would not have wanted to explain the spit on burger or drugged wine. However, I was fifteen and not too swift yet.

The town was pretty well shut down due to the blizzard. I had to make my tracks in the snow disappear somewhere. I remembered that there was a convenience store about a quarter of a mile away that I could lose my tracks in. I could enter one door and leave by the other. In my mind, I had to make it there before the Police tracked me down. I just knew that the police was hot on my heels. I needed a lift to get my feet up out of the snow. That was when I spotted a slow moving trash truck heading my way. I decided to jump onto the back when it stopped at the corner and ride a few blocks ending my trail of foot prints. I quickly made my way to the corner and positioned myself to jump on the back. Boarding was no problem. I had seen trash men hang on the back of trucks my whole life. Much to my dismay, the truck took off and then suddenly sped up and traveled two miles down before stopping. It was a cold ride on the back out of town. I wasn't able to get off till he pulled along the shoulder to let a road grader go by.

Annoyed with myself, I walked along on the shoulder

of what would be a heavy traffic highway if there wasn't a blizzard raging. There wasn't much traffic moving and hitching a ride proved fruitless. I had only counted three fans and I was frozen stiff to boot. I had to count the dude's exhaust fan on his stove. It was a stretch, but I did see it in operation sucking out hot air and smoke. Where was I going to find three more fans before I became a permanent ice cube? Window Peeping has its moments.

As I walked along the shoulder with a foot of snow covering it, a lumberyard delivery truck pulled along the shoulder ahead of me swerving like someone in the passenger seat had a hold of the wheel making it do so. The passenger door flung open and a girl got out screaming obscenities at whoever the driver was. I checked out the advertising on the side of the van and was delighted to see that it belonged to one of the local lumber yards and had a series of three overhead ceiling fans painted on the sides. "Thank God!" I muttered too myself. For once in my life I wanted to go home and get warm. My count to six was up for the night. I was cold and sure that I was going to turn into a frozen corpse if I didn't get out of the weather. I sped walked past the girl heading toward home. I wasn't getting in on her problem, whatever it was. I was too cold.

"Hey, wait up. I know you from school. Let me walk with you till this jerk goes on?"

I stopped, turned around, and waited on her. She would be a good alibi for the evening if I needed to explain where I had been for the night.

"What were you doing riding with that jerk from the lumber yard? Everyone knows he is a pervert." I stated waiting on her. "Girls like you should be careful."

"I work part time at the place. My car was snowed in and the freak offered to give me a ride home. The store manager wouldn't let me go home early like everyone else in town. Did you know that jerk tried to kiss me and fondle me? I slapped him and told him he better let me out or I was going to mace him." She stated firmly showing me a little hand held container of mace."He called me a little . . . and let me out. What is your name? What grade are you in? My name is Jodi Jones. Isn't that a boring name?"

"My friends call me Bump." I replied."I am in the tenth grade and no, your name is not boring."

"I am glad you were out for a late stroll, Bump. It made it easier for me to get rid of the jerk. He recognized you from school. Jerks don't pull things in front of people that know them. Aren't you in a social science class I am taking? My grandmother is going to kill me for riding with him. She told me to stay clear of him, but has never given me a reason. My grandmother is weird and thinks she can read people. I think she is an educated old idiot who expects way too much from me. I am a senior and she expects me to start college in the fall. I have no intention of doing that. I like my job at the lumber yard and I don't see anything wrong with me being just a sales clerk. Somebody has to do it, and I actually enjoy it. I can't see myself wearing a little conservative black pantsuit every day like her. She is boring and her life sucks." She stated pausing to take a breath.

"Do you always talk so fast, ask questions, and spout everything you know in one breath?" I asked starting to walk towards town.

"My grandmother says I speak in overkill mode. The

neighbors call me motor mouth. The teachers at school send me to the office when they have had enough. Why are you freezing your buns off walking on a night like this? Where is your car?" She asked calming down.

"I am sorry to admit that I am just fifteen and not driver's age yet." I replied rubbing my hands together swiftly trying to warm them.

"Well Bump, should you need a ride in the future. I owe you one for walking me into town. I see civilization and the convenience store ahead. Why don't we duck in there for a moment or so and warm ourselves. I'll buy you a hot chocolate. I am in no hurry to get home. I live with my grandmother in the fifth house behind the store, that old Victorian piece of crap. I don't have to be home till midnight."

"Hot chocolate sounds pretty good right now, if you are paying. I am temporarily tapped in the finance department. If you want, I will walk you home afterwards to make sure the jerk doesn't spin around and bother you." I stated trying to extend my time spent with her. She had my heart racing. I think it was her spiked heel snow boots that was doing it. She had on tight jeans stuck down in the top of them. The boots went up to her knees and had a ring of rabbit fur at the top. She looked hot.

"Not a problem," she stated. "I just got paid. I am a working girl."

Five minutes later, we entered the convenience store. After purchasing a couple cups of hot chocolate, we exited the back door of the store and continued our walk toward her place. I wanted to see where she lived. She was beautiful and I felt like a melting snowman. I was flushed and knew that she was the one for me. I fell in love with Jodi Jones when I was fifteen and I am still crazy about her. However, she was seventeen at the time and an older woman.

As we walked, I prayed that my acne wasn't too obvious. I was going to have to pray that the Big Bump Man cleared my face quick and let some facial hair grow in. I would ask Granny Snoop when I met her the next time how to make myself appear at least two years older. I needed help because I had just fallen in love with an older woman of seventeen. She should have heard the rapid beating of my heart. It was making drum sounds.

"That is it!" she said stopping and pointing to an old three story Victorian home.

I knew where I was. Her home was the one I met Granny Snoop at on New Year's Eve.

"Your house looks like a grandmother's house. Do your parents like antiques or something?"

"I live with my grandmother. She got custody of me from my parents when I was about two. I think they owed my grandmother money and she took me instead. They called and asked for a handout once when I was about five. They haven't called since. I just don't understand why my grand-mother didn't send my parents money. She has plenty of it. I heard her tell them over the phone no and not to call any-more. Who tells their son not to ever call? I am afraid she will tell me to get lost and never call when I tell her I am not going off to college in the fall. I might not have a home to come home to after September. I don't want her money, I am making my own. I fear I am going to do something that will cause her to tell me to go away and never come back. I love her and she is all of the family I have. I don't have a clue where my father is."

"Your mouth is in over kill again." I stated as we stood looking at the grand old Victorian that had seen its better days. A rich man had probably lived in it a hundred or so years prior. "Do you have two grandmothers" I asked thinking of my one. I was the offspring of a John and I had no grandmother coming from a father's side of a family. I also wondered if Granny Snoop was related to her.

"I suppose everyone has two grandmothers. Think about it bump, it takes two to tangle. Your mother has a mother and your father has a mother. I actually have three grand-mothers because somewhere I have a stepmother who has a mother. "

I blushed because I felt like I had just failed reproduction class with Jodi Jones as the teacher. I dropped the subject deciding that Granny Snoop had probably been one of the many guests at the party.

"I saw the balloons on your mailbox at New Years. Did you have a big party or something?"

"I didn't hang around. It was an old fogy's party with stuffy glasses of champagne and the fox trot. I climbed out my window and spent the evening with a friend across town. He is a little older than me, but we had a great time. We sat in his hot tub for the evening and then watched a couple movies he had rented. We celebrated the night in our own way. I almost had an accident that night. I forgot my pills. I was New Year's lucky."

I ignored her references to an older dude. I glanced at the snow behind us. Ours were the only foot prints in the new fallen white stuff. In my new perception on life,

I could see our footprints walking out of the snow and thru eternity together. I was in love. Maybe I would say six prayers for her and her over kill mouth to fall in love with me. She definitely had a talking problem. I would try to win her away from the older dude, probably a senior.

"Thanks Bump for walking me home. It didn't seem like such a cold walk having someone to talk with."

"Which one is your window? I might want to toss a pebble at it some night so we can swap stories about how awful our family's parties are. I kind of like the way your mouth runs eighty miles an hour. If I should be in a quiet mood, I wouldn't have to worry about talking. You could do it for both of us." I replied taking the last drink of my hot chocolate.

"The second window on the upper floor is my bedroom. My grandmother goes to bed with the chickens. Yell at me some night or throw a pebble at my window. I will slip out and we can walk down to the convenience store for a coke or something. Just remember, I am never home before ten-thirty due to my working evenings down at the lumberyard."

"Never before ten-thirty . . . !" I replied eyeing her boots again. Somehow, I just knew she had great looking feet in those boots.

"I arrive home at a little after ten, grab a sandwich, and then head upstairs to my room to change." She added pitching the rest of her hot chocolate and handing me her cup. "Don't ever knock on my house door. My grandmother wouldn't be happy with me hanging out with someone younger than me. She is a Victorian prude. Let's keep our friendship on the hush- hush."

"Hush it is and pull close your curtains up there. You really shouldn't leave them open. There are perverts around that could look thru your window with binoculars."

"I can't help it if I am hot and I don't mind making a jerk somewhere happy. Let him look." She laughed.

So, in the month of March that year, I made friends with Jodi Jones. I made up my mind to never window peep at her house. It was a matter of respect. Also, I had promised Granny Snoop at New Years not to peep at that particular house. I decided that Granny Snoop and the Granny of Jodi could possibly be sisters. I kept my promise to both of them and never knocked or peeped. I was a perfect gentleman and always followed Jodi's lead doing what she wanted. I was going to marry her someday. She was my woman and I was treating her right in whatever way I could. However, I never talked about my family or took her home to see where I lived. She was okay with that. I eventually told her why. When I did, she put her arms around me and held me to her. I can still feel the beat of her heart and the sheer bliss of having her hold me. It was a onetime treasured event.

Jodi and I were night owls and hung out five or six nights a week till about three in the morning. Saturday night was the only night she wouldn't hang with me. She always had plans. I knew she dated older guys on Saturday nights, but I tried not to think about it. I had her six nights a week. What more could I ask? On my nights, I would walk her back to her grandmother's house after we tired of video games and junk food. She would slip back in her bedroom on the second floor by climbing up a ladder like flower trellis to the roof of the front porch and then into her window. I always waited and watched to make sure she was in her window except on the nights she had on a short skirt. I closed my eyes when she climbed on those occasions. She was going to be my future wife. I had no business peeping up her skirt till we said, "I do!" It never occurred to me when warm weather hit and we headed for the pool, that I was seeing everything when she wore her bikini bathing suit. Fifteen year olds don't always think too rationally. I closed my eyes on short skirt nights.

Jodi always had money and paid for most of our activities. She was a working girl who knew that I wasn't old enough to earn a dollar yet. She was okay with that. We had a great time together.

At school, she ignored me. It wasn't considered cool for seniors to hang out with freshmen. I was okay with that because I had her when it was important, in the night hours after my peeping.

CHAPTER THREE

THE TEACHER'S LOUNGE

Window Peepers don't just peep into house windows. In high school, boys in their earlier teens try to find ways to peep into the girl's restroom and shower room. We are all window peepers at one time or another. Even you are. When you go to the mall and look into windows dreaming about owning what is on the other side of the glass, you are window peeping. When you glance thru your boss's glass office window to see if he is in there, you are window peeping. When a woman holds up her compact mirror and watches someone behind her somewhere in a restaurant, she is peeping. We all have peeped thru hospital nursery windows at other people's babies other than our own. Some of us just take it a little beyond the ordinary.

Off limits in most high schools is the private lounge of the teachers. Anything off limits calls to a window peeper. I often stood and watched the teachers go in their private lounge and wondered what fabulous amenities they had that we students didn't. I pictured a big screened TV and a monstrous refrigerator with barbecued ribs and potato salad in it. Teachers were fat, they had to eat well. I also pictured a monstrous coffee pot that they possibly spiked. My family was drunks and I just assumed that everyone else hit the bottle a little. I pictured a huge bottle of Vodka sitting next to the coffee pot. At fifteen, you always felt that the teachers were a little off their game in the afternoon. It never occurred to me that some of them were just older and a little slower possibly needing an afternoon nap. To me they were off their game and had to be spiking their coffeepot. That was what my parents did. They spiked everything including their cereal when we had it. Food was not a priority at our house.

The Teacher's lounge and its plain Jane wooden door with no window had my attention and fascination. At fifteen, I was working up the nerve to open it and peep in. There was no way of telling if there was anyone in there or not and that posed a problem. I was trying to come up with a plan for counting those teachers going in and those exiting without being noticed. No peeper wants to be caught. I did not want to walk into the Teacher's lounge to find that it was one huge restroom with open doors and some nude teacher sitting on a stool staring at me. I had no idea what a Teacher's lounge was suppose to look like and I was not interested in teacher nudity. My mother, sister, and grandmother were always spaced out of their gourds and lay around the house half dressed or in the nude. Nudity held no mystery or appeal to me. It was the respectability, nice clothes, and work ethics of the teachers that I admired. Their lunch totes and bags were what I was curious about. I wanted to know what made them special and my mother, sister, and grandmother not so. I figured the clues were in their purses, totes, and lunch sacks.

April and Easter week rolled around. It had taken almost

a whole school year to get up enough nerve to look into the Teacher's lounge. I set a peeping counting goal of looking into their lunch totes till I had a six count of anything that could be considered off the wall. I decided ahead of time that I couldn't open the totes. Peeking was my bag, not handling. I was laying down the ground rules ahead of time. I could peep only in those sitting open. At the most, I felt I might have sixty seconds in the lounge. I had to have a plan and move quickly.

Just before Easter break, I stood across the hall corridor from the Teacher's lounge during class changes and eyed those coming and going from it. From my position in the hall watching teachers come and go, I surmised that there were four folding chairs and a folding table of some sort beyond the entrance. Beyond that I couldn't tell. I guessed that there had to be lockers or kitchenette facilities out of the view of the students. The school definitely wouldn't want us seeing a bottle of Vodka. The teachers were always coming out with mugs of something to drink. They probably had a private stock behind the door. I fantasized that there had to also be lunch totes and forbidden, exotic, off beat adult treasures in there somewhere. My goal was to count six.

I had done my preliminary peeping on Monday morning before school watching teachers enter and exit the lounge. Now, I had to choose a time and a plan in order not to bump into any teachers entering or exiting the lounge. The teachers had to obey the bells just like the students. When the last bell rang, the teachers had to be in their classes or at the least outside their doors getting ready to enter. They handed out tardy slips once they closed their doors. I just had to wait till the last bell rang between classes to peep.

That was easy enough.

When the last bell rang, I would pretend that I needed to tie my shoe, stoop down till the teachers entered their rooms, and then dart into the Teacher's lounge when the hall cleared. If someone was in there, I would apologize and yell. "Sorry, my buddies pushed me thru the door."

Everyone makes mistakes and as a rule, people think it is funny when a man accidentally walks into a Women's Restroom. Women accidentally walking into the Men's Restroom, is equally as funny.

It was mid-morning on the Monday before Easter that I first got up the nerve to execute my plan to peek and count something off the wall in the Teacher's lounge. When the last bell rang between two morning classes, I stooped to tie my shoe and watched the teachers up the hall enter their rooms. The teachers all had to be out of the lounge, so I quickly pushed open the door and stepped in. It was empty as expected. One open topped sack sat on a folding table. Next to it sat a half drank mug of coffee. I walked over quickly and peeked in the sack. To my surprise, a roach ran out. I jumped back and grinned. One of the teachers wasn't too clean at her house. Then I heard a door latch make a sound on the back wall and realized that a bathroom was there and someone was about to exit. I darted for the door, opened it, and ran for my life. At the end of the hall, I darted into the boys restroom leaned against the door, and then laughed. My first attempt at Teacher's lounge peeping hadn't been too successful, yet it wasn't a failure either. I had seen a roach run out of a lunch sack. Carefully opening the boy's restroom a slit of a crack, I peeped to see who was exiting the teacher's lounge. My stomach turned into knots seeing the high school principal walking out.

"Oh crap . . . "I stated realizing I had almost been caught by the big guy. Tomorrow, I would have to pay attention to who went in and make sure that all of them came back out. I didn't realize the principal used the teacher's lounge. I assumed he was the big wig and had his own private facilities somewhere.

After the principal disappeared around the corner, I abandoned the boy's restroom and headed for the office to get a pass to get into class after being late. I told the office girl that I had a serious stomach ache and just couldn't leave the stool according to the bell. She bought it. Who can argue with Mother Nature?

Sitting in the school office waiting for my pass to get back in class, I considered what I had seen. Could a roach exiting a teacher's lunch sack be considered off the wall? Replaying the event in my mind, I decided the sides of that brown paper sack to a roach probably seemed like walls. He did run out and off the sack wall onto the table. So, I counted the event as the first off the wall item seen in the teacher's totes. The roach was a stretch, but I wasn't too picky as a fifteen year old.

On Tuesday, I decided to pull the peeping routine between the last two classes of the day thinking the teachers wouldn't be too interested in keeping their totes closed at that time of day. Lunch and afternoon break times would be over. I was sure the teachers would be a little careless just before going home and the totes would be open for viewing.

Once again, I pulled the tie my tennis shoe routine and waited for the teachers in the hall to enter their classrooms after the last bell. When the coast was clear, I pushed the door open gently and scooted quickly in to find the trash can next to the door over flowing with soda cups, fast food sacks, and foam containers. The teachers ate a lot better than the students. I saw thrown away bits of fries, burgers, and Chinese chicken. Someone had even thrown away a fortune cookie unopened in a little clear wrapper. I retrieved it from the trash and quickly tore off the clear wrapper, snapped it open, and read the tiny paper slip fortune.

Six is your lucky number. Beware of two men.

I grinned and stuck the tiny little streamer of white paper into my jeans pocket. I needed some luck. I didn't ordinarily take souvenirs, but the cookie was a discard and I was hungry. I popped the cookie in my mouth and then pulled a half eaten paper holder of cold French fries from a fast food bag and ate them. There was never food at my house and those fries might be all I had to eat till I returned to school tomorrow. About that time, the fire alarm went off and I quickly exited the teacher's lounge. I didn't want to get caught in there with teachers and students suddenly filling the halls. Everyone in the hall was intent on exiting the building and paid me no attention. I flowed with the masses outside of the school and waited for the city's fire truck to come and inspect the building. I knew which boys regularly set off the fire alarm. That was their thing just like peeping was mine. They were fire alarm handlers who watched afterwards. They were a different form of peepers.

Standing outside waiting for the firemen to do their thing, I thought about the trash sacks in the Teacher's lounge. It never occurred to me that teacher's ate fancy carryout for lunch. Carryout to me was out of date groceries from the food bank once a month. I carried them out and my mother loaded them into our old fifty year old beat up truck. However, I never got to eat much of the carry out from the food bank. My mother sold the food off for cash to buy drug ingredients. I longed to be a man like the principal and eat carryout. The fortune cookie was a real treat for me. I was ashamed of who I was and what I didn't know or have. I would never admit to the kids or my teachers that I ate cold French fries from the trash because I was hungry and considered it my last meal for the day. The only thing on the table at home would be a bottle of wine or vodka.

I considered what was in the fast food sacks and questioned whether there was anything in them that could be considered off the wall? The fortune cookie was the only thing that I could come up with. Getting your fortune told was sort of off the wall. So, I decided the fortune cookie counted. I still had time to fill my quota of six off the wall items in the Teacher's lounge before Easter break. I would keep peeping everyday till my goal of six was completed.

Another school day rolled around. I was yet to look into an actual lunch tote belonging to a teacher. I leaned on the wall outside of the high school waiting to go in. It was a pretty day and I was milking the early morning moment for all I could get out of it. The sun felt really good on my skin. As I stood there, I saw Mrs. Liverpool the Algebra teacher heading toward me carrying a huge blue tote. She weighed at least three hundred pounds. There was no way in my thinking that she could go all day without snacking or eating. That blue tote she was carrying had to be filled with interesting food and other off the wall items. I made a point of opening the door for her and tried to peep in the tote as I did so. It didn't work. She thanked me and then entered intent on getting to her class. I gave her a little space and then followed her. I wanted to see where she was stashing her huge bulging blue tote. Sure enough, she headed for the teacher's lounge and entered. After a moment or so, she came out without it. My curiosity was peaked and I could hardly wait for the last bell between classes to ring. I once more would pull the tie my shoe thing. I had improved my Teacher's lounge peeping plan. I now counted the number of teachers going in before the last bell and then again as they left. That gave me a better idea of whether anyone was in there or not. I had really freaked out the first time when I was almost caught by the school principal. I didn't want to repeat that.

As the last bell between classes rang, I stooped to tie my shoe lace. I was going to get to peep into that big blue tote. I was sure that she had to have something off the wall in there. When the last teacher left and the teachers in the hall entered their rooms, I rose from tying my shoe and quickly entered the teacher's lounge. There was the usual array of thrown away breakfast food sacks and coffee cups. I grabbed half of a breakfast sandwich that was thrown away in the top of the trash and ate it. I was too hungry to be picky about eating after someone. The table had some scattered napkins and a salt and pepper shaker on it. There was a little kitchen area behind the table hosting a small sink and a microwave. On the kitchen cabinet set a red plastic cooler that some people carried a six pack of soda or beer in. I quickly walked around the table to check it out. There had been a lunch in it. Now it was empty except for three little melting ice cubes that looked like three melting glaciers floating in an ocean of cold water. One raisin was floating in the water. I decided it had to be a seal in search of a new home because his Iceland home had melted. I was lost in the fantasy when suddenly I heard a hand on the door knob to the room. Like a shot, I made a dash for the teacher's lounge restroom and barely made it in closing the door when I heard footsteps enter. Then I heard one of the folding chairs pull out and someone sit down.

I instantly locked the door and broke out in perspiration. There was no way in hell that I was going to open that single bathroom door till whoever was out there left. I sat down on the stool to wait patiently. When the person on the other side tried the bathroom door handle, I reached over and ran some tap water so they would know the John was occupied. I glanced at my watch. I had been in the teacher's toilet facility for ten minutes. Then a knock came at the door.

"Are you going to be in there much longer? I have got to get back to the office." A male voice stated.

I was in trouble. I had been sent to the office often enough that I recognized the principal's voice. I looked down at my feet shaking my head. To my surprise, there sat that big blue tote of Mrs. Liverpool's beneath the lavatory. I peeped in the top and saw that there was a pregnancy kit in the top. I wanted to laugh, but now wasn't the time. The teacher with the big blue tote was single. My mother and sister had thrown enough of them in the bathroom trash can over the years that I knew what they were all about.

Once more, the principal knocked and spoke. "I really need in there. I think I have the stomach flu and I need to go bad. Could you please hurry?"

Raising my voice to as high of a pitch as I was capable of at the age of fifteen, I stated."I can't come out right now. I am Miss Liverpool and I am in the middle of taking a pregnancy test. Could you use the student's restroom, please?"

"Er . . . uh . . . sorry. I'll come back later." The principal's voice stated from beyond the door.

I was relieved to hear him leave. Afterward, I didn't waste any time getting out of the teacher's lounge. I first peeped out the bathroom door and then the hall door. When I saw the principal disappear around a corner, I flew down the hall and into the boy's restroom once more. Peeping back out, I saw the principal and Mrs. Liverpool heading for and entering the teacher's lounge along with the office receptionist. I leaned against the bathroom door and sighed. Then I quickly exited and made my way to the front office to once more ask for a hall pass to return to class.

The nurse, this time, took me into her office and asked if I might need a laxative. She suggested that she thought she should call my mother and suggest it to her. I grinned and told her to go ahead. My mother would be drunk and probably not even answer the phone. My mother started drinking and doing drugs at noon and was smashed by the afternoon. The nurse gave me a pass and I returned to class.

Sitting in science class, listening to the teacher drone on and on about what made up the composition of dirt, I considered what I saw in the teacher's lounge. It was a stretch again, but a seal swimming alone in a lunch tote with a three melting glaciers was sort of Sci-Fi. I counted it as number three. Number four was the pregnancy kit and my time spent looking at four bathroom walls sweating it like a pig. Now, I had two off the wall items to go.

My last class of the day arrived. I thought about making another trip to the teacher's lounge after class to peep, but decided against it since the teachers would be congregating there claiming things from their lockers. I noticed that Mr. Barker, my English Teacher, had already claimed his things for the day and had a big brown sack sitting with its top open on the floor in front of the blackboard. It had to be his lunch sack. I had to find a way to go to the blackboard and take a casual peep into the top of the sack and hope that there would be something off the wall in it.

Fate always comes thru. Mr. Barker asked for a volunteer to go to the blackboard and copy the questions from a sheet he was holding up onto the blackboard as a study guide for an upcoming test. My hand flew up, in spite of the fact that my handwriting was not the best in the class. Surprised, Mr. Barker called me up to the front and handed me a page with eight questions on it and a piece of chalk. I started on the left of the board and wrote the questions each time peeping into the top of the brown sack as I went stepping around it to finish each sentence. The first pass over it, I saw that there was a piece of cloth in the brown sack and that an odor was coming from it. By the fourth pass over, I had decided that the fabric looked like a pair of underwear. On the sixth and seventh past, I surmised that the odor was like that of a baby diaper. Then, I heard the teacher sneeze and make a run for the door. On the eighth pass over, I realized that the teacher had a problem for the day and had come to school sick with the trots. The sack probably had held his lunch at some point during the day, now it held his soiled underwear. I grinned and finished writing the eighth question on the blackboard and took my seat happy as a Lark. Pooped in underwear in a lunch sack was definitely off the wall. That was number five.

It was at that point that I reconsidered visiting the teacher's lounge after school. If I could peep in one more lunch sack and find something off the wall and crazy, I could go to sleep in peace that night and not have to go out and peep in windows. Jodi had told me earlier in the day that we would not be able to hang out together after ten-thirty because her Grandmother was insisting she go with her somewhere overnight. It was rare that I didn't see Jodi after window peeping. However, it would be nice to have one night at home to wash my bed sheets and clothes.

The water and electricity were on at my house which was a rarity. I needed to wash my clothes and bed linens while I had the opportunity. My parents weren't good about paying utility bills. It wasn't unusual for us to catch rain water off of the roof to flush the stool or bathe with. I tried to shower everyday at school in the boy's locker room slipping in on the end of the last PE class headed for the showers. I couldn't remember the last time my mother washed my clothes or cooked for me. I never peeped in houses like mine. Respectability and a higher class of family were what I dreamed of and peeped at. I hated everything about my drunken parents as well as my life.

After school, in an effort to peep one last time in the Teacher's lounge, I hung out in the boy's restroom till the hall cleared of teachers and students going home. I waited about twenty minutes or so. When I was sure that the hall was vacant, I walked quietly towards the Teacher's lounge door, stopped in front of it, and looked both ways. I didn't see or hear anyone anywhere. Quietly, I opened the door and peeped in to make sure the lounge was empty. To my surprise it wasn't. I peeped in just in time to see my principal, Mr. Smith, kiss the janitor, Mr. Lewis, on the lips having him pushed up against the wall in a compromising position. The fortune cookie's prediction flashed across my mind. "Six is your lucky number. Beware of two men." I quickly let the door slam shut and ran for my life hoping they hadn't seen me. I made a quick decision while sprinting that I was a believer in Chinese fortune cookie predictions. Everyone believes in something. To this day, I guard my fortune cookie when eating the oriental stuff. I don't want the Chinese Psychic Gods upset with me.

I sprinted till I was outside the school and then slid behind a huge campus oak tree to hide. Panting, I tried to control my breathing while at the same time laughing. I was lucky to be alive and sure that the two men would have killed me had they seen or caught me. I decided at that point, Teacher's lounge peeping was not a healthy choice and swore off it. After a few minutes of leaning on the tree, I took into consideration what I had seen. The lunch room or teacher's lounge was like a huge lunch sack the teachers ate from. It was a stretch again, but an educated principal being attracted to an uneducated janitor was off the wall to me. Different social classes in my book didn't mix. Granny Snoop didn't come to my house to socialize. She was educated. We were not. I had seen men kissing many times in my peeping thru windows. It was the class distinction of the two men in my mind that was off the wall. Keep in mind, I was just fifteen and knew nothing about love or attraction.

Happy having completed my six peeps into teacher's lunch sacks, I stayed home for the night, did my laundry, and totally ignored the drunken rants and yelling of my mother and grandmother as well as the crying jag my drunken sister was having. At night, when I was small, I would count to six over and over in my head as I went to sleep to drown out the verbal abuse and drunken voices of my family. Six was as far as I could count when I first started. Repetitively counting to six, as a first grader, had been a sleeping pill. Now, it has to be peeping at six items or people. Afterwards, I can sleep never hearing anything around me including fire trucks, street traffic noises, or my mother's voice.

I have a screw loose and it was my parents that loosened the nut.

CHAPTER FOUR

TWO PEEPING TOMS

It was the first Saturday in April and Easter weekend. Jodi never hung out with me on Saturday nights. I was cool with that. I wasn't old enough to ask her to marry me yet. I was a pimpled faced sophomore and lucky to have a senior chic as beautiful as her hang out with me. I wasn't rocking my boat because she chose to date other older guys on Saturday night. I knew I had it good. She and Granny Snoop had become my pretend family. Someday, I would introduce them when the time was right.

My real home was a place I slept, cooked boxes of macaroni and cheese when there was any, and tried to stay out of the way of a house full of drunks who weren't past taking a skillet or a chair leg to me. My family was on food stamps, but my father or mother usually sold them for liquor or items to make meth with. My meal in the cafeteria at school was the only meal I had most days. I worked in the kitchen at lunch running the dishwasher for it. Jodi didn't realize that the candy bar or hot chocolate she bought me at midnight was the only food I had ate since lunch. I was a skinny little ninety eight pound sophomore with dreams of someday being normal like the people I peeped at thru windows. I also dreamed of facial hair coming in so I could grow a mustache and look older for Jodi. She liked men with mustaches and beards. I wasn't sure why.

Saturday night was my serious peeping night. Granny Snoop usually had an invitation for the evening and I would make a point of meeting her at a back window somewhere at exactly nine. She was very social for an old lady. She got around. Sometimes, when she could, she would sneak me a saucer of party goodies into the bathroom and hand them out the window to me. I tried all kinds of unusual snack foods thanks to her. A new world of eating opened up to me and I developed a taste for exotic foods that would never have crossed my plate at home. She gave me a taste for the foods of a higher class of people.

I had told Granny Snoop that I might not make it to meet her on the Saturday night before Easter because that was my major night of peeping for the spring at the mall. She said she understood. I explained to her about the different women's stores I peeped in. She was interested and told me she wanted to hear every detail of my adventure when we did get together. On this particular pre-Easter Saturday evening, she said to meet her if I had a chance, but if I didn't she would understand. We always met at exactly nine on Saturday nights for a ten or fifteen minute chat thru a window. It was an odd relationship, but it worked for the two of us.

The mall is the place to be on Saturday afternoon before Easter. Practically every woman, young or old, is there trying on new Easter dresses. Boys rarely join the frenzy of Easter clothes shopping. They are usually happy to wear whatever and slide thru the day of fashion craziness. Women are different. They can't be seen in just any old thing. Even my drunk of a mother and grandmother sobered up enough to shop for a dress or hat for Easter. They were Catholic and attended church on Easter if they were sober. The rest of the year they didn't give God a second thought. They didn't give me a second thought the rest of the year either.

Being a peeper, the mall is a treasure trove of places and people to check out. Sometimes in the larger chain stores, when the crowds were huge and the staff was short, I would watch for the women's dressing rooms to fill up. Then, I would pull a garment on a hanger off of a rack and approach the clerk who was too busy to care about much of anything and say, "My mother yelled from the dressing room that she got the wrong size. May I take this back there real quick and hand it to her? I see how busy you are."

"Sure, go ahead." Most of them would say totally ignoring me.

So, I had permission to enter the women's dressing room. I would saunter back to the fitting room with a dress in tow and knock on the first door not saying anything. The door would open and two thirds of the time there would be a lady or a girl standing there in her slip or half dressed in something she was trying on thinking it was the sales clerk checking on them. Before the girl or woman behind door one had a chance to scream, I would quickly say in an apologetic voice. "I am so sorry; I thought my mom was in this cubby. " Usually, the woman or the girl just quickly closed the door and I moved on. Then I would go down two or three dressing room doors and pull it again. After the third time of knocking, I would quickly find an empty stall, enter, lock the door, and then hide out till that set of women and girls cleared out. When the fitting room filled up again, I would come out and pull the same peeping scam working my way back out of the women's dressing room. Once in a while, I got a little screech or a 'You're too old to be bringing your mother items back here." I always just grinned and agreed with them stating I had told my mother the same thing. As a rule, I knocked and peeped in three fitting room stalls going in and three going out which made my six for the evening.

On the Pre-Easter Saturday when I was almost sixteen, my mother in one of her non-drinking moments decided I needed new trousers to attend mass and drug me off during the afternoon hours to the mall where we ended up in the men's section. She picked out three pairs of trousers she thought were suitable for mass and sent me back to the men's dressing room to try them on. I wasn't the only unhappy teen boy and man back there being forced by a woman to try on Easter duds. I found an empty dressing room stall second from the front. I had just kicked off my tennis shoes, dropped my jeans, and was standing in my boxers when a knock came at the fitting room door. I flung the door open thinking it had to be the male clerk handing me another pair of trousers sent back by my mother. Too my shock, it was a cute girl with her hair up in a ponytail and she was holding a dress shirt on a hanger.

She quickly stated, "My dad yelled from the dressing room door that he had picked out the wrong size shirt and asked me to bring him the correct size. I am so sorry! I thought he was in this stall."

I grinned, snorted, and shut the door thinking she had possibly made an honest mistake. Then I heard her work two more doors on down and I broke out laughing. I was a Peeping Tom who had been had by a Peeping Angel. I didn't leave my fitting room stall. I just remained quiet. My mother had said she was going to wander over to the dress department and would be back in about twenty minutes. I put back on my jeans and tennis shoes and waited.

Sure enough, in about twenty minutes I heard her start working back down the stalls spouting the same routine. Thinking I was gone, she knocked. Opening the door quickly, "I screamed at the top of my lungs and the clerk came running and I told him what she had pulled. He grabbed for her and she ran. I played the poor innocent kid that had been peeped at. It got me a free T-shirt from the department store. I was happy with that. It wasn't often that I got new clothes.

(Let me throw in at this point, when Easter morning did roll around, my mother was drunk as a skunk and the trousers never saw the inside of a church. She returned them to the mall when she had a sober moment and bought cigarettes with the money. I would have worn the trousers to school if she had let me. I only had two pair of jeans and both of them were two year old rags. Wouldn't it have made more sense for her to have traded them for a pair of jeans for me? Drunks and addicts are self- centered.)

After returning home with my mother from the mall and eating a rare Saturday lunch due to her being sober, I decided to return to the mall later to peep after she and my dad dove into their usual Saturday night bottle. I would have to walk the couple of miles to the mall because I didn't have bus fare. That was okay. It was springtime and the late afternoon was beautiful.

As I walked across town, I made mental note of certain houses that might be good ones to return some night and peep in. I never peeped in the lower class, dump part of town. What the poor people had was not what I was interested in. I peeped and dreamed of a better life.

Arriving at the mall, I entered and started to walk flowing with the crowd of Easter window shoppers. You can peep at a lot of crazy things walking along the glass lined store fronts. Window shopping is probably the only legal form of peeping. I recognized a couple of other window peepers as I walked the length of the mall and then back again. You recognize the traits of a peeper, because you are one.

Legally, I watched teen girls trying on jewelry thru the front window of a cheap jewelry shop. At the hosiery shop, I watched women buying pantyhose and other items holding them up to inspect and down against their legs to check the color. I watched women in children's clothing sections bend over to check on their children in strollers, hiking their rears in the air like targets. That is legal peeping when you are on the outside of a mall window looking in from the corridor. I spent hours watching girls trying on Easter shoes. I watched mothers trying on respectable dresses. I purposely watched thru windows at the ones that I wished were mine. I didn't look for a grandmother in my peeping. As far as I was concerned, Granny Snoop had filled that empty place in me.

Peeping into the women's restroom at a mall is almost impossible. If I had an urge that I wanted to do so, the direct approach was what I took. I would just walk straight in the door and while I was taking a quick glance, I would state, "Oh shit . . . I am in the girl's restroom," turn and run out. Everyone would just assume I had made an honest mistake. If I got in there and no one was in sight, sometimes I would hide in one of the stalls till six women would come and go and stand on the stool so they couldn't see my male tennis shoes. When it was clear, I would quickly exit without washing my hands. In some situations like that, it is okay not to wash your hands, especially if it means you might get arrested by mall security. If I felt the women's restroom was especially filthy, I would then go in the men's restroom and wash my hands. A peeper has to do what is best in the situation at hand.

I had been at the mall for several hours peeping when my stomach started growling. I really didn't have any money to waste on food. I had two one dollar bills that was the change from paying for my trousers earlier in the day. The store clerk had handed me the change instead of my mother. I had stuck the two bills and change into my pocket. My mother forgot to ask me for it later and I didn't mention it. I rarely had money. Two bucks wasn't much, but it was enough to get me a soda or something. Usually, I would sit down with a family at the food court. Sometimes, they wouldn't clean up after themselves and I would eat or drink what was left. Anyone seated in the area just thought I was with them and lagging behind. I always cleaned up to make it look like I was with them.

It was about eight or so in the evening when I stopped in front of a cookie shop to peep thru their window. I watched as a baker in the rear picked her nose and then rolled out cookie dough. Had I peeped at that same nose picker thru someone's kitchen window, it would have been illegal. I stood lost in thought contemplating the legal and illegal forms of nose picking when I spotted the ponytailed Peeping Angel from the men's fitting room wandering around in the sweets bakery. I wondered what her game was.

Amused, I watched her. She had probably been at the mall

all day, was hungry, and planning to swipe something to eat. She had that look. In my mind, I quickly decided she had to be a thief as well as a peeper. I stood legally peeping thru the storefront window. She walked around the store looking like she was sniffing all the baked goods. I was sure that I eventually was going to see her lifting something. She continued to walk with her hands behind her back sniffing the merchandise. I just had to know what her game was. So, I took the couple bucks from my pocket and entered the store and purchased one cookie hanging onto the receipt to prove I wasn't in on her game if she tried to involve me. I stuck the receipt in my shirt pocket. I sat down at one of three little tables in the shop, nibbled at my cookie, and watched. It wasn't long till she sauntered down the aisle by the table where I was sitting.

"Peeping was your game earlier, what is it now?" I asked her in a low smirk of a voice so the bakery clerk couldn't hear.

"Shush . . ." she stated putting her finger to her lips. "What in the hell are you doing here?"

"I am eating a cookie. What are you doing here? Aren't men's dressing rooms more your style?"

"Shut your mouth you little jerk." She stated putting her finger to her lips. Then she quickly flashed a policeman's badge clipped to the belt in her jeans that was hidden under the sloppy high school logo T-shirt she was wearing.

"Where did you steal the badge?" I asked to annoy her. "You can't be over sixteen."

"I am twenty-two, a cop, and yes I look sixteen." She whispered in an annoyed voice. "Now cool it and don't you move. I was looking for a pervert working the fitting rooms earlier in the day."

She then continued to wander around the end of the rack and then scared the pee-wad out of some twelve year old kid who was filling his pockets with prepackaged, individual cookies. When she had him by the arms and was trying to cuff him, I jumped up and ran like hell. I didn't stop till I was outside of the mall. I hadn't done anything wrong, but I was taking any chances. I didn't have a record at that point and I knew my parents would literally beat me if I brought cops to our home address. They were meth dealers and laid low.

The cookie was a good, chocolate chip.

CHAPTER FIVE

QUESTIONABLE CRÈME AND DENTURES

After fleeing the mall, I checked out the time on my watch. It was half past eight. I had plenty of time to make it where Granny Snoop was spending the evening if I hurried. We had an agreement. If I didn't show up by five minutes after nine at the window of wherever she was snooping, she would go her way knowing that for some reason, I couldn't get there. After a miss of seeing her, I would check out the bulletin board at the convenience store. She always pinned up a note on the lost animal bulletin board with the words "Looking for Dog named Bump". She then would write a street address with the number written in reverse and a date written in reverse informing me where she would meet me the next time. That was our only means of communication. I didn't want her to know my family, I was ashamed of them. Apparently, she didn't want me to know hers. That was alright with me. Our system of communication worked and I looked forward to our short visits which sometimes weren't but about five or ten minutes long. People were always inter-rupting us, wanting in the bathroom.

Tonight, she was going to be at a male friend's house for dinner. I wasn't quite sure why she wanted to visit the old fart that lived at the address on her note. I recognized the address and had window peeped there on previous oc-casions. He was an old white headed dude with a beard, who wore dentures and a hearing aid. He used that men's hair coloring stuff to turn his beard and hair a funny shade of brown. When I was that old and ugly, I was going to stay indoors and leave the ladies alone. I was not going to make a fool out of myself chasing some young skirt. I didn't have the heart to tell Granny Snoop that the old guy was seeing some younger female. I had never seen her, but once when peeping thru his bedroom window that he left cracked because he smoked cigars, I heard her talking to him from the bathroom about what was going on at the high school. Her textbooks were on the end of his bed. There was no hope for old perverted, hair colored farts in my fifteen year old thinking. He had one leg in the grave and his teeth had already been buried. I couldn't imagine what some young chic saw in him.

Fifteen year olds don't always get what they are seeing. I didn't at the time. A girl high school age shouldn't have been in his bedroom or his shower. All I was concerned about was pondering why Granny Snoop was interested in spending the evening with him, much less check out his medicine cabinet. I knew what was in there; butt crème, denture paste, and high blood pressure medicine. I had watched him take them out of the medicine cabinet on a previous peeping occasion. I couldn't image what her at-traction to him was. However, she wasn't me and I was sure she had her reasons. She was a peeper and handler of things. Maybe his medicine cabinet of crap intrigued her. Handling someone else's butt crème, however, was a little off the wall to me.

The neighborhood was in walking distance and I sped walk to get there on time. I made my way to the rear of the house at the address she had given me. It was a fairly nice neighborhood with sidewalks and manicured lawns. I could picture kids playing at night chasing fireflies and families barbecuing and having friends over to sit on their patios. I longed for normal and dreamed of barbecued burgers.

Barbecuing at my house did not produce food. My mother placed foil wrapped rocks on our barbecue grill to look like baked potatoes. It was a cover to hide the meth cooking in my father's old falling down, paint peeled shed he called a garage. My mother always kept four hamburger patties made from a cheap can of dog food in the refrigerator. On the side of the barbecue grill she kept a bottle of barbecue sauce with half a bottle of cologne mixed in it. When cops showed up inquiring about a smell, she let them smell her barbecue sauce covering the smell of the meth. If cops appeared suddenly, she grabbed the dog food burgers and threw them on the grill and poured the cologne sauce on them. The cops usually went away shaking their heads thinking my mother was a horrible cook. I hated my life with my parents. When I graduated high school, I was going out on my own and live a normal life on the respectable side of town.

I managed to circle the old fart's house without any one seeing me and stooped below the rear bathroom window waiting. At exactly nine, I eased up to peep in. I saw Granny Snoop enter and lock the door behind her. I tapped on the glass and took a quick glance around the bathroom for the item I had chosen for the night before Easter scavenger hunt. I was counting houses that had Easter towels displayed. This old fart didn't know what a decent decorator towel was. I saw one ragged old green one hanging. It had lost its color and had at least three holes in it. If I was normal and respectable like him, I would at least have a decent towel hanging in the bathroom for myself and one with rabbits or something on it for a chic who might want to hang with me for the weekend. He hadn't made any effort for Granny Snoop. That annoyed me. She was worth a pink or purple towel with Happy Easter written on it. I had seen ones like that at the mall. My Granny Snoop deserved respect. He was a disrespectful old fart. I shook my head once more wondering what she saw in him.

I watched as Granny Snoop did a quick scan of the contents of the medicine cabinet and then opened the window quietly to chat with me. She lit one of her little cigars. I objected to them and gave a quiet fake hacking cough. At least she didn't drink or do drugs. She was a definite step up from my parents or maternal grandmother who was sitting at home at the kitchen table eating pig skins and drinking beer.

"How is your night going?" she asked grinning and handing me a handful of individually cellophane wrapped Easter Eggs from her black pantsuit pocket.

"Thanks Granny, I am sure this is probably the only Easter treat I will be getting unless I lift some candy somewhere." I stated.

Instantly, I saw the disappointment in her face.

"Now Bump, peeping is one thing. However, stealing will get you some serious prison time. Promise me you won't take up stealing. That would break my heart."

"Don't worry! I was just running my mouth. I intend to be somebody when I am grown. I am a peeper, not a thief. How is your night going and why are you spending the evening with the old fart who lives here who has false teeth, dyed hair, nose hairs, and uses butt crème'? "

"I can't be too picky at my age, Bump. Dinner invitations are sometimes few and far between. Sometimes, I have to hint and get myself invited like I have here tonight. I am a drop in guest who showed up at half past eight. A thirty minute visit, meet you at the window, and I am good for the evening. How do you know he wears butt crème and dentures?" she asked grinning and taking a puff of her little cigar.

"I worked this street last summer. I think it was July or august when I did a little peeping thru his bedroom window. He wears white boxers, scratches his backside like a baboon, takes his teeth out, looks at them, and then drops them in a glass of water on his nightstand. He has to be some type of idiot. What if he wakes up some night and thinks the glass is a fresh glass of water. He could drink that food crap crud that is floating off his dentures. God forbid you should spend the night with him. He might set that glass on your side of the bed. Can you see yourself being confused in the middle of the night and drinking his denture crud?"

"You definitely have made a point, Bump! I will make sure that I don't sleep here or ever with him. The denture glass I could put up with, but I am not fond of a man who wears white boxers. I am a colored boxers' woman, the brighter the better."

I laughed at her comment thinking she had to be some woman to look over the denture glass. "Good for you, Granny Snoop. I personally prefer a woman in pink underwear like the girl that sleeps with him on Saturday nights." I replied pausing and then added, "I shouldn't have said that. I am sorry."

"How young of a girl sleeps here on Saturday nights?" Granny Snoop asked taking a puff of her cigar and the smile on her face fading.

"I have never seen her face, but she arrives here on Saturday nights after ten-thirty. Her legs look a lot like Jodi's, a high school friend of mine."

A knock sounded on the bathroom door, "Are you alright Georgia?"

"I've got to go, Bump! The old fart, as you call him, is getting antsy. Thanks for telling me about the girl in pink underwear. I owe you one."

"Dump the butt crème user!" I replied. "I really think you can do better!"

Granny Snoop smiled at me and said, "I use the stuff too. It is part of growing old."

"Oh!" I replied. "Well, at least have your own tube. He could have some funky germs in his."

"Your point is well taken. I definitely will purchase my own tube of butt crème. Thank you for watching out for me. I will always remember this night and your magic words about a girl wearing pink underwear and the old fart's tube of butt crème. You will never know what your words have meant to me. They have cleared up a mystery for me."

"My magic is you, Granny Snoop. You and a girl I am in love with are the only good things in my life besides school. It was magic the night I met you. Did you know that you are my best friend? Just don't ever tell my girl if I bring her around."

Granny Snoop looked at me with a serious expression on her face. "Thank you, Bump! I have got to go or the old fart is going to break down the door. You have proved your friendship to me by telling me about the girl in pink underwear. Does she keep clothes here? I would like to peep at them."

"I think I saw him hang a blouse of hers in his closet the night I peeped."

"Thanks, my friend bump, I really owe you for this one and I definitely will peep in his closet before this visit is over. I will wait till he goes to the John."

Granny Snoop closed the window and prepared to open the door for the old fart to see that she was okay. I intended to go home with Granny Snoop and live with her if she ever asked. I was okay with living on the fifth floor of an old person's apartment complex. She had told me once that was where she lived.

I longed to escape the drug house existence of my parents. They didn't care enough to feed me or give me lunch money for school. I never remember them helping me with my homework. Even though I did poorly in school, I loved going. It was a safe haven for me. I wanted to learn and be someone. My poor grades were from staying up all night to avoid my parents' drunken outbursts and drug dealing. I was surviving till I was old enough to kiss my meth lab home goodbye.

I day dreamed about Granny Snoop asking me to live with her. I fantasized about her making me a bed on one of those fold out couches. I would do the dishes everyday and earn my keep so she would never have a reason to throw me out. Her couch was okay with me, if she offered. Her one bedroom apartment in an old folk's hi-rise would be heaven compared to life with my family.

CHAPTER SIX

PROM TIME FOR JODI

May rolled around and it was prom time. Jodi was a senior and really excited about picking out a dress and the accessories that matched. She went on and on at night about the event and her upcoming shopping adventure with her grandmother to purchase a gown and shoes. She was a talker and I rarely had anything great to talk about, so we were compatible. She talked and I listened. I liked her mouth that was always in overdrive.

I knew that Jodi dated older guys on Saturday nights. I was okay with that, but down deep I dreamed she would ask me to go with her to the prom. I saw us as a couple, even though we had never kissed or anything. I just hadn't got up the nerve to try yet. We hung out six nights a week after ten-thirty. How much more steady do you get than that? I wanted to go to the prom with her. I was almost sixteen and I was starting to see myself as a man, Jodi's man.

Two weeks before the dance, a senior jeep driving stud asked Jodi to the prom. She accepted and I was pissed.

However, she was all I had to hang on to in my world of nothing so I decided to suck it up and not give her any indication that she had hurt me by not letting me go with her. She was mine six nights a week and I wasn't rocking my boat. She and Granny Snoop were everything to me and I felt that I couldn't exist without either of them in my life. I loved them. I listened to her go on and on about the Saturday night prom, her date, and the perfect dress she was envisioning. I kept reminding myself that I was lucky to be hanging out with her. I was from the wrong side of the tracks with nothing to offer her. Jodi was gorgeous enough to have any high school stud she wanted and she had chosen me six nights a week. I just prayed that she would one day give me seven nights a week and make me her one and only man.

About ten days before the senior prom, Jodi's grandmother went with her to the mall to pick out her dress. That night, I threw a pebble at her window to let her know I was there so we could go play the arcade games. She excitedly held her dress up in the light of her window on the second floor for me to see. It was red. Who in the hell wears a red, slinky, form fitting, low necked, strapless, mini skirted dress to a school prom? I was expecting a floor length pink, purple, or possibly blue ball gown. In my thinking, the very short, red, strapless dress was a whore's dress. I had seen my share of hookers in red dresses buy drugs from my parents. I was not happy about her choice.

After Jodi climbed down from the second floor, she asked me excitedly what I thought about her prom dress. Perhaps in the back of my mind, I wanted to get even for her going with someone other than me to the dance. I lost it. My mouth went into overdrive, a first for me. I told her that she had disrespected me and all of the nights we had spent together by not asking me to go with her to the prom. Then I proceeded to tell her that if she had asked me, I would not have taken her to the prom in the cheap red hooker dress she chose. I was pissed and definitely lacking in words of tact. I even went so far as to ask her if she purchased the dress at a thrift store. I made it very clear that I thought it was a cheap whore's dress.

She was pissed then. After calling me every male ego degrading word she could think of, she told me to take a hike and never talk to her again. Then she climbed back up to the window of her second floor bedroom, slammed the window down, and closed her curtains. I was in the dog house of all dog houses. My nights after ten-thirty with Jodi abruptly ended.

Needless to say, I made a big mental note in my forming male brain to never tell a girl you hated her dress or that it was one that a whore would wear. Harlot opinions could cost you big time and were best kept to yourself. I made up my mind to tell her she looked great in no matter what she wore once she started speaking to me again. She was everything to me. I didn't want locked out of her life. After a week of her ignoring my pebbles pecking her window, I decided I was willing to crawl and tell her I loved her hooker dress. Boy . . . was I willing to crawl.

On prom night, I stood in the shadows near her house and eyed the dude in a jeep who came to pick her up for prom. She still wasn't speaking to me. Her date was definitely a senior and on his way to getting drunk. I watched as he drank from a bottle before going to the door for her. I pictured him as my dad at that age. That was probably how my father started his spiral downward into the world of being a drunk and a druggie. If I ever took a girl to the prom, she would be safe with me. There would be no alcohol or drugs.

The dude went inside after knocking on Jodi's door. It wasn't long till he exited with Jodi on his arm. She was wearing the skimpy red dress and she looked damn hot in it. Maybe my opinion had been a little hasty. The high school wasn't but a quarter of a mile down the road. I decided to make my way there on foot and peep at the prom for my night's scavenger hunt adventure. I needed six of something to peep for. I was sure that Jodi would probably be the only prom date there wearing a red dress and red spikes. So, I decided to look for five other females wearing red hi-heels to make a six count. The jeep sped away and I started walking towards the high school. I was green with jealousy but there was nothing I could do about it. Apparently the love of my life didn't see me as prom material. I was from the wrong side of the tracks and poor. Maybe she would have been embarrassed to be seen with me. I had a big pity party as I walked. I felt like my heart was in my shoes.

Jodi had a reason for not asking me to her senior prom. We all have secrets that we wished would never be found out. She had hers and I just hadn't discovered what it was yet. It would break my heart, but not stop me from loving her. I loved Jodi Jones and still do.

The May night was warm and the sky was studded with stars. I didn't want to think about the jeep dude and what he might do or try with Jodi after the prom. In my thinking she was a virgin. As a male, I was aware of what the senior boys expected. I listened to them in the boys' restrooms at school brag about what they had planned for prom night.

I hoped it wouldn't be a night of regret for Jodi. However, I would love her and forgive her of anything.

Peeping in at the school gym at the prom was not a problem. The gym doors were propped wide open with a couple of rocks. I wasn't the only underclass male peeping at the gorgeous girls. I recognized a classmate of mine from English class. I wasn't sure what his name was. I kept to myself as a rule. No one wanted to be friends with a ragged boy from the wrong side of town like myself. I didn't have clothes, money, or anything in my mind to offer anyone in the way of friendship. I was lonely as hell and depressed about Jodi.

The guy I recognized was just as small and wimpy as I was. He wore big black glasses that hid his face. He was sitting outside the entrance on a retaining wall watching the couples go in. He was dressed nice in trousers, dress shirt, and tie. However, he looked really uncomfortable and kept fiddling with his clip on tie. I decided to be friendly and sit a while with him on the wall. There was plenty of time to peep and count red high heels. The night had just begun.

"What's up?" I asked sitting down next to him on the wall and pulling my legs upon the wall and crossing them Indian fashion.

"My parents are what is up. They have insisted I sit out here for the duration of the prom dance and make sure my sister, who is a senior, is okay. They don't approve of the guy she is with."

"I gather her date is not a prize in your parent's eyes." I stated feeling I wasn't a prize in Jodi's eyes.

"He was the only one that asked my sister to the prom. My parents should lighten up a little bit. Jill, my sister isn't exactly God's gift to men."

"My sister is no prize either. She's a drunk who recently got fired from the airline she worked at. What is your name? I know you are in my English Class but we have never hung out."

"My name is Jack." The small framed boy replied.

"What class are you in?" I asked making small talk.

"This is my junior year. I will be a senior and out of here next year. What about you?"

"I failed a year and am a year behind. I am currently trying to pass the tenth. Hopefully, I will be a junior when you are a senior. I am sixteen or will be in a few days. How old are you?"

"I will be seventeen in August. I am a few months older than you."

"Why are you sitting out here? Juniors can attend the prom as long as they ask a senior girl."

"I am on God patrol according to my parents. I am the eyes of God making sure that my sister remains pure and holy. Going to a dance in our family is almost considered a sin. My parents are religion freaks who drive me and my sister nuts with their dos and don'ts. This isn't the first time I have had to play chaperone for my sister. I am not happy having to watch her strut around in hi-heels. I had plans to go to the movies."

"Well, at least your parents care about her and you. "

"They care enough to make our lives miserable. My dad

broke his leg this afternoon is the only reason she is getting a little slack. He intended to chaperone. I am here, but I don't intend to watch her. I am just going to sit, enjoy the music, and then ride home with them when they come out. One more year, and I am not putting up with any of my parent's bullshit. I have just about reached my limit."

"Your dad is probably trying to save your sister from a night of regret. There is a lot of drinking, drugs, and sex after these dances. Your sister will probably be safe, no regrets, and tucked in her bed when the rest of the world is going crazy tonight."

"Why are you here?" he asked.

"A girl I hang out with is in there on the arm of a jeep driving dude. I have been a little pissed that she didn't ask me to come with her. I will admit I am spying on her. She has on great red spikes and looks hot. Would you like to hang with me for a couple of hours and do a little peeping at red spikes?"

"Will the couples be able to see us?"

"They will all be too busy dancing, hugging, and smooching to pay us any attention. You can tell your parents that you kept a close eye on her and not mention how many gorgeous girls' cleavage you have looked down at." I stated standing up relinquishing my position on the wall.

"Would it upset you terribly, if I looked at the guys in the Tuxedos?" Jack asked with big questioning eyes as though he were testing my willingness to hang out with him.

"No, being gay is fine with me. I know about girls born into male bodies and males into women's bodies. I don't have a problem with however you see yourself."

"I have one year of school left and then I am going to move far, far away and live a life as Jackie. I am a girl in a male's body. My parents will never accept me as anything but a male. They are Sodom and Gomorrah preaching freaks. My dad is a Baptist minister."

"Your secret is safe with me. Call me by my nickname which is Bump. What do you want to be called?"

"How would you feel about calling me Jackie? My real name is Jack but the girl in me would like to be called Jackie when I am out of my parent's sight."

"Well, Jackie, come on. Let's go peep at some ball gowns and tuxedos. We might as well make the most of the evening while you watch your sister and I spy on Jodi. I am going to marry her someday when she discovers that I am a man."

Jack or Jackie seemed pleased that I was willing to hang out with him and we headed for the side of the building to peep thru a window that was about six feet off the ground. I showed him how to climb up the cinder block wall like it was a rock wall and then balance himself holding on to the window ledge. He seemed shocked to find out that he could do it and was really pleased with himself. I made a new friend a week before my sixteenth birthday. Little did I know how important that friend would be to me.

Up to that point, I had kept to myself because I was poor, pimple faced, and from the wrong side of town. I found a friend who was equally as withdrawn for other reasons. We became secret pals. He never visited me at my house and I never went to his. We were best friends where it was safe for both of us, at school. I was hiding from alcoholic parents and he was hiding from religious ones.

The prom dance wasn't offering anything too exciting to keep my attention. After twenty minutes hanging at the window, I had counted my quota of five pair of red high heels to go with Jodi's making six. Jackie was getting equally as bored hanging at the window.

"What do you say we do a little car peeping and maybe scare the pee wad out of a couple or two?" I asked letting go of the window ledge and dropping to the ground.

"It sounds like a winner to me. My sister hasn't tried to sneak out the back door with her date or anything." He replied and then added. "I wouldn't tell if she did. I am sure she plans to move out next week as soon as she gets her diploma. If she doesn't, she is crazy."

"Good, come on." I stated and we started running around the school building and then slowed down to quietly walk up thru parked cars and limos in an effort to catch someone necking. First on the list was a shiny red convertible with a couple openly necking in the front seat. We crept up to the back of it and just stood and watched biting our lips to keep from laughing. The couple was oblivious to our watching them. The guy's tie was off and the girl had tossed her shawl of a thing into the back seat along with her tiny evening bag. I wondered what in the world she had in the bag. It was too little to hold much of anything. If it had been open, I would have made a point of peeping in. However, it was closed and I was not a handler of things. Jackie seemed more interested in watching the dude.

Nudging Jackie with my elbow, I pointed to a motorcycle parked on down where a prom couple was getting on the cycle in gown and tux. Jackie grinned and pointed to a yellow two door auto a couple of rows over where a couple was necking. The windows were down and the radio was playing. Quietly, we crept to the rear of the vehicle and once more stood in silence watching the couple's choice of necking ritual. The guy had his arms around her waist. She had her arms around his neck area. One of the girl's hands was wrapped around the neck of a bottle of wine. I saw my mother and dad in them. They were on their way to getting drunk and entering the land of regrets. Neither of them would remember prom night tomorrow. They were spending it in a bottle. I was sure that my mother had no memories of me as a baby or a toddler. When I was born, my mother was high and drunk. I don't know why social workers let my mother take me home. For a brief moment, I imagined myself being conceived on Prom night. Then I told myself not to fantasize. My maternal grandmother had made it clear to me on more than one occasion that I was a bastard child whose father was a John.

After watching the prom drunk couples neck for awhile, I spotted the jeep belonging to Jodi's date. The jeep was rocking, so we sneaked up on it. I was secretly jealous and pissed. I intended to bang on the sides and make a scene. When we approached the jeep and peeped in, I was surprised to find the dude with a girl in a yellow prom gown necking. I stepped back and laughed from sheer relief. Jackie gave me a funny look and then we ran because the dude in the jeep spotted us and was climbing out of the jeep half dressed to kill us. I would definitely ask Jodi about her prom date when she was speaking to me again. She should have asked me. I wouldn't have traded her in for the yellow dressed chic. The half dressed, barefoot dude didn't chase us too far. We easily got away and slid behind a van probably belonging to a teacher and laughed till we almost cried.

"Did you see his boxers with cartoon characters all over them?" Jackie asked laughing.

"Did you see her awful yellow dress?" I returned laughing. "She looked like a stuffed yellow Tulip."

After a short round of snorting and laughter, Jackie put his fingers to his lips and pointed to a red four door family car parked a couple of rows over. It was rocking and the windows were all steamed up. I followed his lead and we sneaked up beside the four door compact motel room on wheels. A pair of red spikes sat on top of the car that looked a lot like Jodi's. Whoever was inside the car had apparently been barefoot and sat them up there till they were finished in the love making department.

Jackie put his finger to his lips and then lightly removed the spikes from the top of the car. I watched quietly not sure of what he was up to. Then, I followed his lead and we walked a couple of rows over and he sat down on the ground leaning against a bumper. I joined him. He removed his men's loafers and socks. He then proceeded to put on the red open toed sling back spikes. I grinned thinking he had pretty nice looking feet for a boy. A little nail polish and his feet would look pretty good in those red beauties.

"What do you think?" he asked extending his legs out in front of him and moving his feet around to look at his feet in the spikes from different directions.

"Red is definitely your color." I replied. "If you had your toenails painted, you would have some hot girl looking feet."

"Really?" he stated all smiles.

"You should definitely always wear spikes when you start your new life somewhere. "

Jackie got up and attempted to walk in the four inch spike heels. It didn't take long till she had them mastered. I picked up his loafers, stuffed his socks in them, and followed him thru the parking lot as he pretended to be a model walking down a runway. I could tell this was a rare moment for him to be himself and he was making the most out of it.

"Come on! " I called after he was finished with his runway modeling. "What do you say we go back and shake the red compact and see who the girl is that wears such hot shoes? The windows are still steamed up. Why don't we shake the car and then yell police to scare the devil out of them." I stated in a low voice putting my finger to my lips again. I placed his loafers on top of a car so we could go back and easily find them.

"Wait." He stated leaning against a car and starting to unbuckle the straps of the red spikes."

"Wear them!" I stated putting my hand on top of his and stopping him from taking them off. You can return them to the school lost and found tomorrow. You probably look better in them than she does. "

Jack grinned at me like I was the first person in the world that had ever recognized him for who he truly was, a girl. He twirled around a couple of times doing a little dance number in the spikes. I saw a spark of who he wanted to be, a woman. I was okay with him discovering himself. My day would come and I would escape my nightmare and become who I wanted to be.

Walking quietly in heels is not an easy thing to do. Slight

repetitive click sounds echoed from the parking lot pavement as we approached the red compact. The red compact was rocking. I was sure that whoever was in there wasn't paying outside sounds any attention. It was Prom night. There would be a lot of cars rocking.

Jack pointed to the steam on the windows. Grinning, I followed his lead. We both put our hands on the hood of the car to rock it when we were ready. The car windows were fogged over and we couldn't see who was inside. Just as the car was rocking a little slower, we hit the hood hard with our hands, bouncing the car, and yelling "Police . . . . .!" Jack immediately started backing up knowing he would have the hardest time running having on spikes.

To my horror, the doors flew open and Jodi with the old fart Granny Snoop knew came scrambling out of the back seat of the car. He was half undressed. Jodi's dress was half off of her.

"Run," I shouted sprinting to Jack's side. I grabbed his hand pulling him along and we ran for our lives. I knew if Jodi caught me she would pull every hair out of my head. She had seen me and I knew that I was dead meat. I didn't even think about what the old dude might do."

Jack was laughing, running, and squealing like a girl. I kept hold of his hand. I wasn't about to let him get caught by them. I was the one that told him to keep Jodi's spikes on. Just as we ran around the back of the school building, Jack stumbled and one of the red spike heels broke off. I stopped, helped him up, put the broken spike in my pocket, and then we dashed behind the school dumpsters to catch our breath. I knew the old dude would not follow us very far because he was half naked. However, we needed to get Jack's shoes. I decided to wait twenty minutes and then go back for Jack's loafers and socks. I could run faster by myself if the old dude was still hanging around looking for us. There was no need of both of us getting killed.

Both of us were trying not to laugh or make any noise as we stood behind the dumpster. I could hear Jodi in the distance screaming at me that she was going to kill me when she caught up with me. I was going to have to lay low for awhile when this was over. I knew I was on Jodi's crap list but good and that was one floor below the dog house. I was now in her dog house basement.

"I gather you know her?" Jack asked giggling and breathing hard.

"That was Jodi. She hasn't been speaking to me because I told her the red prom dress she chose was a whore's dress. Now I know why my words made her so mad!" I stated in shock."She is one. She was making love to a man who was at least sixty or seventy.

"Whore is a little harsh, don't you think? She is probably just different like me, Bump. A whore works seven nights a week. Didn't you tell me earlier when we were hanging out at the window that she spends six nights with you? If I were guessing, I would say she is in love with that older man and can only see him one night a week. Maybe the old dude has a family or works nights. You are right about the dress though. It is more appropriate for a thirty year old. Maybe she is trying to dress older for him just like you would like to grow a mustache and look older for her." Jack stated giggling.

"So, in your opinion she isn't a whore?"

"No, she is just in love with an older man. She does have great taste in shoes. I am going to hate returning these, especially since I broke the heel off one of them."

"I will return the shoes, Jack. She is my friend. I will tell her I did it."

"You would take the heat for me?" Jack asked big eyed.

"You are a girl! Of course I would take the heat for you." I returned grinning. Somehow, I knew that my new friend Jack needed me to see him as a girl. That was alright with me. He needed a friend as much as I did.

"Thanks Bump. This has been one of the best nights of my life. Thank You for accepting me as Jackie!"

"How about you forget your sister and I will walk you home? If you want, I will call you Jackie when we are in private."

Jack smiled so big that I could swear I saw his soul.

CHAPTER SEVEN

ARREST OF THE JUDGE

Jackie's words ringing in my ears, I decided to give Jodi the benefit of a doubt. Perhaps she was just in a passing faze of infatuation with an older man. I could live with that. She was the love of my life and I was willing to let her have her present moment of madness. I was sort of in love with Granny Snoop in my own way and she was as old as the butt crème user. Maybe the old dude was filling some missing part of Jodi. I wanted Granny Snoop in my life. Maybe that was how she felt about the old fart. I would wait a few days and then apologize about the dress, shoes, and the car shaking. She would eventually see the humor in it all, I was sure. After all, we were meant to be together. She just didn't see it yet.

Just to be sure, however, I was going to follow Jodi and see if she really worked part time out at the lumber yard for the next week. She did have lots of free money that she spent on me. I hoped it was legitimate. I was suddenly enticed into peeping into the private window of the girl I was in love with. I decided to spend the next six nights following her. I had to know for sure that she wasn't a hooker. I could live with the fact that she was having an affair with a married man. I didn't think I could live with her being low life like me and my family. I needed to admire her.

About one in the morning, Jackie and I went our separate ways. We had sat on the curb a couple doors down from his house and got to know each other as he waited for his sister to arrive home and then chaperone her into the house. It was after one in the morning and I walked away into the shadows of the wee morning alone. I decided to go check out the old fart's driveway and see if he and his red compact car were home. If he was home, then I knew that Jodi was safe in her bed on the second floor of the old Victorian house behind the convenience store. I was sure that he wouldn't take Jodi home with him knowing how young she was. More and more, I felt that I needed to keep track of Jodi. I could be a leach if she would let me. However, she might stomp Bump the leach if she caught up with me tonight.

I had to walk, but in about thirty- five or so minutes I made my way into the neighborhood of the old fart. There was a lot of activity on the street for the time of morning it was. As I neared the old fart's house, I saw that there were a couple of cop cars and an ambulance parked in the old man's drive. I sauntered up and joined the crowd standing along the curb and asked a man in his pajamas what was going on.

"The old dude apparently has been seeing a high school girl and she is a minor."

"Why are all the police and the ambulance here?" I asked standing with my hands stuck in my jeans pockets.

"It is illegal for a man his age to sleep with a minor. He is being arrested."

"Oh . . . ! " I stated suddenly comprehending the situation. "Do you know the girl?"

"Apparently, the teen girl is his sister's granddaughter. I don't have the full details. The girl must be his great niece."

"The old man has a sister?" I questioned.

"She is the older woman sitting in that cop car over there." The stranger stated pointing.

I looked in the direction he was pointing and all the blood drained from my face. Surely this nightmare wasn't happening.

"Oh . . . shit!" I replied starting to put two and two together. "Where is the girl?"

"She is wearing that red dress over there. She is cuffed to a social services officer. She tried to run."

I stared into the shadows and saw Jackie in her infamous red dress standing cuffed to a woman cop who was keeping track of her.

"Why is there such a big deal being made of this. The girl looks like she is about eighteen. "

"The old guy is a big shot here in town. He is a judge."

"He is a judge" I asked in shock realizing that he and Granny Snoop must have been trying to set me up for possibly a peeping sting. I wondered in the moment if Jodi was in on a plan to take me down.

"He is a juvenile court judge. She is a psychiatrist who works for social services."The stranger stated.

"Oh . . . I see." I stated not asking any further questions. However, I suddenly felt like a fool. I was sure that Jodi and Granny Snoop had both played me for an idiot.

Granny Snoop was Jodi's grandmother and she didn't live in a hi-rise old people's apartment complex downtown. She lived in the big Victorian house that I wasn't allowed to knock on the front door. My heart was in my shoes. Neither of the women in my life had been honest with me. I felt betrayed.

"There will be some juicy gossip when this hits the morning paper." The stranger stated laughing. "Who are you, anyway? Do I know you?"

"I live a couple of streets over. I am out looking for my dog that got loose. Have you seen a yellow collie?" I asked. I had learned early as a peeper to use that excuse when peeping in strange neighborhoods late at night."

"No, I haven't seen your dog. However, he could have wandered past here in all of the excitement and no one saw him. It isn't every day that you see a judge bite the dirt for raping a minor and incest with his niece."

"So the judge is her uncle?" I asked in shock.

"A distant one . . . ," The stranger replied."You should have seen the older woman swinging a handgun around earlier. She had the judge on his knees in his pajamas on the front lawn while she was dragging her granddaughter out of the house with her other hand. She has guts. I heard her calling the judge a perverted child molester. She threatened to shoot his thing off. His reputation is toast."

I realized at that point that Granny Snoop wasn't my friend. She had played me for information about the old fart. I had told her practically all of my secrets including the facts about my parents being drug dealers. I had trusted her. She pumped me for information about the old fart and the girl in pink underwear. She had used me. My heart was in my shoes. I wondered what kind of game she was playing. She set her brother the judge up to be arrested. She probably was setting me up for a future sting as a window peeper. She lived with Jodi in the big Victorian house behind the convenience store, not in a hi-rise. She had lied to me. Did Jodi know who I was and that was the reason she wouldn't let me knock on the front door? Was she in on Granny Snoop's deception?

"What will happen to the girl?" I asked fishing once more.

"The girl will go to the hospital for a rape kit and then be sent to Juvenile hall for the night. The judge, on the other hand, is being arrested and will have to make bail. He is going to be one pissed snake tomorrow. He will probably try to talk his sister and niece out of pressing charges to save his reputation and ass."

"The old woman didn't know he was sleeping with her granddaughter?" I asked fishing one last time for information.

"The old lady showed up with a cop, opened the door with her key, and all hell broke loose."

The crowd was starting to disperse because raindrops were starting to pepper the neighborhood where we stood. I couldn't get involved and have the police ask what I was doing in the neighborhood. I walked away into the shadows of the night. I would check out the morning newspaper for the details of the night. I decided at that point that I was never speaking to Granny Snoop or Jodi ever again. I had to live with my parents and I couldn't bring law enforcement home. I had nowhere to go.

After thirty minutes of walking towards home, my head cleared a little. I decided that the next night I would climb up to Jodi's second floor window and have it out with her. If she beat me and half killed me over the shaking of the car bit, I would just take it. I was sure I couldn't live without her in my life. I had to know if she was in on Granny Snoop's game with me. I loved Jodi Jones. I decided I could forgive her for the old fart. I wasn't sure I could forgive Granny Snoop for using me. I would stay clear of her.

My confrontation with Jodi never happened. She disappeared after leaving juvenile detention the next morning. Missing person posters were plastered all over town and the state. Many speculated that the judge had done away with her to keep her from testifying against him. However, there was no trace of her and no one could prove she was alive or dead. I stayed clear of Granny Snoop dropping off of her radar. I didn't retrieve anymore notes from the convenience store. My world and the women I loved bellied up.

I turned sixteen two days after the prom and just a few days before my tenth grade school year ended. My mother and father were high on meth on my birthday. There was no birthday cake, party, or present. No one remembered me except Jackie. She slipped me a birthday card with two movie tickets in it during our shared English class. I wrote her a note and threw it at her when the teacher wasn't looking telling her I wouldn't use them till she could go with me. She grinned from ear to ear. Fate had brought me a new friend to take the edge off of my broken heart. Jodi was missing and presumed dead according to the paper. I was in a time of grief and needed Jackie's friendship just as she needed mine.

Jackie's gift of movie tickets opened a whole new world to me. I saw beautiful exciting lives on the movie screen and a new safe haven to sit in. I was a peeper and the huge movie screen was a new adventure. After two or three visits to the movie theatre, I found a way to slip in thru a service door. I really didn't have money for movie tickets and I was hooked. Some nights I didn't peep. I would watch six movies in a row starting at noon. Six movies and I could sleep.

When Jackie could manage, I sneaked both of us in to the matinees. His parents never allowed him out at night. He pretended a need on Saturday afternoons to visit the library and then would meet me instead. He also discovered a world that was denied him. He liked the love stories or chic flicks. Even though Jackie was a very short, skinny small boy, he was nine months older than me and going on seventeen. He would be a senior next school year and going to prom. He told me he dreamed of being the girl and going with a tuxedo man. I was alright with that. He told me everything he hoped and dreamed for including a life on the west coast living as a girl and not a guy. He wanted to be a hairdresser.

Jackie clung to my acceptance of him. I was an accepting anchor that he desperately needed. I was a good listener and a friend. He told me everything. I, on the other hand, could never bring myself to tell him that I was a window peeper. He was maturing and didn't sleep with stuffed animals. I, however, needed the peeping like it was a stuffed toy. I couldn't go to sleep without it to cling to. I didn't want to look wimpy or needy to him. He needed me for a friend and the girl Jackie in him needed me even more.

CHAPTER EIGHT

JACKIE'S PROM

A year passed. The end of my junior year was approaching and the end of Jackie's senior year. I continued to peep and sleep on rooftops to avoid going home anymore than necessary. Jackie became my close friend and filled my loneliness. Prom time had once more arrived and this time it was for Jackie. At school, I called him Jack. In private, I called him Jackie and treated him like a girl. He was one. I hadn't given prom too much thought because I wasn't a senior yet and I was still in love with Jodi. The girls at school just didn't interest me. I am a one woman man and Jodi was my heart. Somehow deep inside me, I just knew she wasn't dead. At least, that is what I wanted to believe.

By the middle of my junior year, I dropped the Jack and just accepted Jack as Jackie my best friend. She was a girl and I treated her as such. We bonded and there came a point that I no longer cared if she had a male body. I called her Jackie at school and wherever we were. What the kids at school thought didn't much matter to me. They had never been there for me in my Hell, Jackie had. She was my friend and she was a girl. So, it was prom time and

Jackie was doing the girl chatter thing about ball gowns and tuxedos. I just listened and agreed with her. I had learned from my experience with Jodi to not criticize a girl's taste in prom clothes. I wasn't making that mistake twice. I only had one friend now, and that was Jackie. I wasn't about to lose her. Last year, I had lost two friends; Granny Snoop and Jodi.

There were only a couple or so gay men in our high school that were not closeted. Jackie had asked each of them to go with her and they had turned her down stating they were taking girls to please their parents. Every mother in our town wanted that prom picture to show off, especially if your son was gay and you were denying it. If you had a photo of him taking a girl to the prom, you could deny he was different or God forbid, homosexual.

I had spent a year hanging out with Jackie and after some serious soul searching; I decided that Jackie was a girl just like any other girl in our school. Dealing with the fact that she had a male body, I told myself that she was a female soul that had jumped into the wrong sexed baby when she entered Earth life and was stuck with it. I told myself that it was sort of like putting on a costume at Halloween and then not being able to take it off. No one would want to walk around in a zombie or a Frankenstein costume for a lifetime. Jackie had a Halloween costume that she was stuck, a male body, and she was being forced to wear it year round. She wanted out of it, but that was impossible.

When I came to terms with the fact that she was a chic living in an unwanted male costume, I started treating her as a girl and not a male. Her family was homophobic and forced her to participate in all sorts of male activities from scouting to male service organizations. She did not fit in and lots of the time was ridiculed and made fun of when her parents weren't around. I accepted Jackie as a girl and we spent endless hours on Saturdays at the mall watching chic flicks and endless hours of window shopping at dress and women's shoe stores. She didn't purchase anything, because she couldn't take it home. When I had money, which was rare, I bought her copies of teen girl magazines and she stored them in her locker at school. I wasn't an expert on how to treat a girl or woman, but I tried to treat Jackie like I saw men in the movies do. I had no home role model to pattern my treatment of women after. I did my best to treat her respectfully and for the friend and chic she was. She knew I was in love with Jodi Jones and respected that. We were friends. I was a male and she was a girl who always walked around in a male costume.

It was the night before the senior prom. Jackie and I were hanging out at the mall. Her mother was insisting that she rent a tux for the prom. She didn't have the heart to tell her parents that she didn't have a date. Prom was a major deal for Jackie and she was about in tears for most of Friday evening as she tried to convince herself to enter the tux rental store and pick one out. Her parents were going to force her to go, even if she went alone or God forbid took her sister Jill to make an appearance and get the prom photo.

"I don't know what I am going to do, Bump! I can't show up at the prom with my sister. I am tired of the hide in the closet game. I want to go as a girl to the prom and with a guy just like every other senior girl. I can't help this male body I am stuck with." She stated as she thumbed thru a rack of ball gowns. I could see in her eyes how much she wanted to go to the dance as a woman and not a man.

"You can always change into one of these gowns after you get to the dance. Rent one of each." I suggested as I waited patiently on her.

"That sounds great, but who I am I going to dance with or have the dreaded photo made with. You are the only straight arrow that I know that accepts the fact that I am a girl."

"If you can't find someone to take you tomorrow night, we will go and peep thru the school gym's windows like we did last year." I replied unthinking.

Jackie got the funniest look in her eyes and I knew that I had stuck my foot in my mouth.

"Do you really see me as a girl and a friend, Bump?" she asked unsmiling. "Or am I just someone you have hung out with because you are like me and have no friends?"

"You are a girl and you are correct. I hang out with you because I have no friends. However, my not having friends is by choice and for reasons I don't want to go in to." I replied thinking of my alcoholic parents and the dump I lived in. I never intended to make friends and take them home there. Friends would eventually expect to visit you.

"If you were a girl in a male's body and I was a straight arrow, I would understand and take you to the prom in a ball gown because friends are there for each other in the good times and the bad or embarrassing times. Apparently, I am just a good time friend to you, one that will peep in windows and do stupid stuff. The prom is my bad time and I need a friend."

"I cannot take you to the prom, Jackie. I am in love with Jodi and you know it. I am a one woman man and I am faithful to her."

"What about being faithful to a friend? Do you think buddies should stick together?"

"You and I hang all of the time. I would say I am faithful to you as a friend."

"I have attended a lot of marriage ceremonies at my church and watched couples promise to be there for each other in the good and the bad. Tomorrow night is my bad. I am not asking you to take me to the prom because I don't want to know if you are a good time only friend. When I catch a bus for California next week and kiss this place goodbye, I want to remember you as a friend I have treasured. I don't want to remember you as one who divorced me as a friend when the going got bad."

"Even if you ask me, I can't take you to t he prom, Jackie. In the first place, I don't have the rental fee for the Tux. Plus, I still have a senior year to put in. You know how prejudiced our school is. I would be treated as gay next year."

"I think I am ready to go home now." Jackie stated with a depressed sound to her voice." If you don't mind, I think I will catch the bus home alone. Perhaps tonight and now is the time for us to say good bye and move on. I am used to people pretending to be my friend. One more disappointment is just a little more icing on my cake. I really have thought you were my friend and saw me as a girl and not some gay freak you would be ashamed to be seen with."

"Come on, Jackie. You are putting me in an awkward position. That isn't fair of you." I shot back following her out of the rental evening wear store.

"Peep thru the gym window with someone besides me. If I am not worthy of going inside my prom with you, I sure as hell am not going to settle for a second best experience and peep. Good bye." She stated with a tear rolling down her cheek. She then turned and left the rental store.

I threw up my hands and let her go. Chocolate, she needed chocolate. I would take her some the day after prom and make up with her. Till then, I would stay clear of her because I definitely wasn't going to put myself out there as being gay. I was seven-teen in a few days, a straight arrow, and in love with Jodi Jones.

About eight that night, I started my evening of peeping. My parents were half drunk and in one of their obnoxious run at the mouth, trip over chair stages. I thought about what Jackie said about the good and the bad. My parents lived constantly in the bad and by choice. I, personally, didn't know how they could stand each other. I didn't like them nor did any of the neighbors. I had spent seventeen years dreaming of being free from them. I didn't drink, smoke, or do drugs. One more year of high school and I was out of their life kissing them goodbye just as Jackie was kissing her family and our town good bye. I just needed to survive one more year. I felt it was unfair of Jackie to expect me to make my life even worse for her.

I needed a theme for my peeping for the evening. Bad times had taken root in my brain, so I decided to peep thru windows till I saw six couples that were into bad times. A few days away from turning seventeen, I had just about run out of ideas for themes. This would do for the night. Even though my parents were high, yelling obscenities, and being asses; I would be able to sleep ignoring them because I had counted to six. I had a screw loose and I knew it. I was older now. Breaking the counting bit was going to be hard when I was on my own next year.

There was nothing happening in the first house I peeped into. Apparently, the owners had gone out and just left a light on to make it look like someone was there. I moved on to equally as uninteresting second and third houses. My game seemed to be a little off. Why did Jackie have to go and cry? Her tears earlier were bothering me.

On my fourth try, I peeped into a window and saw a couple put a physically handicapped child to bed that was my age. I could see the older man, who had to be his father, struggling with the dude's dead weight and his elderly mother push a wheel chair out of the way. I was sure they had to love the child they were caring for even though he was grown and too much for them now to physically handle. After the handicapped man about my age was in bed, I watched them kiss him goodnight. He didn't respond. Then the man put his arm around his wife with an expression that read," We have done it one more time." I also read in his face that he wasn't sure that he could do it one more time tomorrow. He looked really tired and so did she. I cringed at the thought that they had shared a lifetime of good and bad and possibly the bad was an everyday one sapping their physical strength. If they weren't there for each other in the bad, I wondered if either of them could have stood alone and cared for the guy my age. From what I was seeing in the window, it was taking both of them in the bad to function.

I moved on. In the next house, I watched an older couple sitting at their kitchen table counting pills and putting them in one of those little seven day plastic divided containers. The man had plastic tubing wound around his ears and oxygen going into his nose thru the tubing. The woman had a patch over one eye like she might have just had cataract surgery or something. I watched her. In spite of the fact that she was seeing with only one eye, she made a cup of coffee and a sandwich for him as he counted pills. They were in a bad time. Illness or surgery was definitely not good times. On the back wall behind their kitchen table hung a photo of them. It was a picture of him as a dashing young military man and she was young, beautiful, and hanging on his arm. Both of them were all smiles. I could see from the photo that they had their good times when they were young. Now, they were experiencing their bad and they were hanging in there. They counted as bad times number two. I moved on.

I hit another house with no luck. There was a man in dirty boxers snoring on the couch. On the floor next to him sat three empty beer bottles. I moved on. I hated drunks.

At the next house, I peeped in a kitchen window that had the window pushed up and open. Apparently, they didn't have air conditioning. I watched as a young couple inside discussed bills that were spread out on their kitchen table. I heard him say, "We are in debt over our head. We are going to have to move out of this rental and in with one of our parents." Then I heard her say, "You are willing to do that?" He replied, "Together, babe, we can make it thru anything including my mother's bitching and your mother's vegetarian refrigerator. Six months of saving and we can enjoy the good times again. We are going to have to suck it up, make it thru this little down spiral, if we want good things to happen for us. Six months and we should be out on our own again."

They counted. Anytime you purposely entered a bad

time and stuck it out together that meant something. I never wanted to return to my parent's house. I couldn't imagine taking my woman there to stay for six months so that we could get ahead. This couple was showing guts in their bad time. I admired them. They were number three.

I thought of Jackie and felt really guilty. All of our time together as friends had been good ones till this prom thing rose up and bit me in the ass. The tension between us and her telling me good bye was definitely a bad time. I asked myself if I was hanging in there in the bad time. I knew what the answer was.

A couple streets over, I peeped into a window and saw a couple each with a newborn baby in arm rocking them. They had twins. I grinned. There were two rockers in the nursery and they both were manning one. Both babies were crying like there was no tomorrow. I had heard about babies that screamed because they had allergies to milk. My mom had told me in one of her few sober moments that I had been a colic baby and she didn't think I would ever shut up when she brought me home. She told me that dad would get up and leave just so he wouldn't have to listen to me cry. I watched as the couple shared the two infants screeched. After a few moments they switched babies but neither walked out and abandoned the other. They just continued to rock and try to soothe the two newborns. Having two screaming infants had to be a bad time. I was sure that both of them would rather have been out back in their hot tub or watching their big screen. I could see that they were in it together and that this night was one of their bad times. The sharing of screaming babies was number four.

I moved on down the street and stopped in at a convenient store to use their facilities. As I was waiting in the back for my turn at the one stool restroom, I overheard a young couple counting their money to see if they had enough money to buy diapers and share a soda. No one likes to drink after another person, not even couples. Spending your last dollar on baby diapers and then sharing a soda was on the bad times scale in my book. Jodi and I had never shared a soda and I was in love with her. I saw in that moment that sometimes you had to do things that might be less than desirable in bad times. I was sure that the young couple would one day be loved by that baby they were sacrificing for. Maybe sacrifice in bad times had its rewards. I could see that they were not drunks and that they were putting their baby and its need of diapers first. They were going to be respectable, good parents and their child was going to be spoiled rotten when the good times hit for them. Sharing a soda counted as number five.

Leaving the store, I made my way into the housing district again. I spotted a house with a lighted window that didn't have the drapes drawn. I walked up to it after looking about and making sure that no one was watching. Then, I peeped in. I wanted to laugh, but I didn't. A woman had a sewing machine out apparently making a new dress for herself. She had her husband standing on a stool with it on and she was hemming it. I thought to myself that he had to be really hen pecked and watched quite amused for a few moments. She stuck him once with a pin and he jumped. However, in spite of the stick, he continued to stand there and let her do her thing. Then I gave their moment some consideration. The woman was saving them money by making her own clothes. It was no more than right he share in the money saving project. Wearing the dress didn't make him any less of a man. He was still a man inside the costume she was hemming. He wasn't the dress. However, I was sure that he would get a lot of ribbing from his buddies if they happened to drop in on him at the moment. Then I thought of Jackie in her permanent male suit that she couldn't take off. The man stood in a dress that wasn't him. Jackie lived in a body that wasn't her. I counted the shared experience sewing couple as my sixth sharing of bad times. They were saving money and he was there doing his part.

It was about midnight and way too late to go to Jackie's house and try to apologize for being a jackass. It was time for me to suck it up and prove my friendship and be there in the bad time. Now, where in the hell was I going to come up with the money to rent a tuxedo and purchase prom tickets? I would definitely be asking Jackie to the prom come morning. I was sorry that I had almost abandoned her in the bad time. I did not want to be my father.

Returning to my house, I found my parents passed out. My grandmother was equally as drunk in her bedroom moaning and groaning. Sleeping on the couch was my only option since my air line stewardess, failure of a sister had returned home. I was surprised to find her asleep on the couch instead of my bed. I headed for my bedroom which was actually a back lean-to porch that had been closed in. My closet was a metal rod hanging from the ceiling in one corner held up by a short piece of chain on each end like a porch swing. My sister had overtaken it with her things. I was a little pissed and started throwing her clothes off of it. That is when I spotted two dry cleaning bags and I knew instantly what was in them. My sister, before she got fired, dated a pilot. In one bag was her stewardess uniform including her hat and in the other was the Pilot's uniform and hat. Suddenly, I had a light bulb moment. Jackie and I could do our own thing and outshine all of the phonies in tuxedos and gowns. We would go to the prom as a Pilot and his stewardess. I couldn't wait till morning. I had to ask Jackie tonight so she would have time to shave her legs and find shoes to go with the outfit. I left my house and walked the three quarters of a mile to Jackie's house carrying the dry cleaner bag with the stewardess outfit in it. I tapped on her bedroom window softly till she woke and came to it.

"It is three in the morning, Bump. What is up?"

"I have come to ask if I can take you to the prom." I stated holding up the garment bag with the stewardess outfit in it.

"You mean it? You will go with me?"

"Here take this'" I said handing her the dry cleaning bag. We are going to your prom as a pilot and a stewardess. You will have to find your own spikes to go with it. We should standout like royalty amongst all the predictable gowns and black suits. You know I am a foot man. I want your legs shaved and your toe nails painted." I stated grinning at her.

"My parents are going to kill me, but we are on. Pick me up at seven. I won't be at school tomorrow. I am going to have my hair done and get a manicure just like all of the other girls. Thank you, for supporting me in my bad time. I won't forget it."

"You are a girl, Jackie. I am going to take the fallout whatever it is next year and you and I are going to dance the night away and have the prom photo made. However, your mother is probably not going to show it to her friends. Just keep in mind, I am in love with Jodi Jones and always will be. This is a matter of respect for the friendship between us."

"It takes a real man to stick around in the bad times. Thank you." Jackie stated excitedly taking the dry cleaning bag. "Here take this to buy the prom tickets. I just got my allowance."

I took the money, but felt really bad about it. She was a girl and I was taking money from her. I wasn't fifteen anymore and willing to let Jodi treat me. I wanted to be a man and take care of the women in my life." I will pay you back the prom ticket money someday, Jackie. I promise."

"What is mine is yours, Bump, no questions asked."

I smiled at her. She jerked her head and the dry cleaning bag in the window because the front porch light came on. Someone had heard us. I ran and hid behind a huge oak tree a couple of houses down. I knew her dad would not be happy if he caught me at her bedroom window at three in the morning. When the porch light went back off, I walked home happy with my decision to be a man in bad times.

On the following evening, I knocked on Jackie's door looking sharp in the pilot uniform and hat. I borrowed dress shoes from an old man down the street that I occasionally mowed grass for. I looked sharp. My sister was drunk when I left and never realized what I had on. Surprisingly, I found a hundred dollars in the breast pocket of the pilot's jacket. I left it there. I wasn't a thief, although it was tempting. I never had any money.

Jackie came running when I rang the door bell and quickly left with me. I understood! Her parents were about to go into homophobic overdrive seeing her in female clothing and spikes. I had a taxi waiting. I wasn't one of the rich kids who had cars or rented limos. The old man who loaned me his shoes advanced me forty on mowing his lawn for the summer. He came thru for me. I see now, he was a friend that I didn't see. Jackie and I left his parents staring and in tears. His younger sister, however, gave us the thumbs up. Jackie was gorgeous. She had her hair and makeup done professionally at the mall. She looked stewardess perfect. Her legs were shaved and her feet looked hot in a pair of navy blue spikes to match her uniform. I was pleased. She was a number ten in the foot department and otherwise. As we closed her outside door, she whispered that she had told her family she was gay when she returned from the mall with her makeup and nails done. I was proud of her.

At the prom, we danced every dance and I held Jackie close like they did in the chick flicks. I moved her around the dance floor like the stars did in the movies making her stand out amongst the cookie cutter prom dates in ball gowns. A couple times, the prom crowd cleared the floor for us and watched us dance in awe. Jackie and I had spent a year watching chic flicks and dancing in the alley afterwards. The other senior guys had spent too much time watching horror films. They had no moves and all eyes were on Jackie and me. I gave everything at prom my best shot and attempted to give Jackie a night to remember. We were the hit of the dance floor and several of the straight dudes seeing she was the hottest chic there tried to steal her away and dance with her. She told them all the same thing, "Sorry, I am flying only with my pilot tonight. He is my goodtime man."

We were hot and Jackie knew it. She was all smiles all evening. When it came time for the prom photo, I put my arms around her and held her tight with my face next to hers. She was my friend, one of my loves, and I was determined to give her a night to remember. I was a straight arrow, but her friendship meant more to me than my reputation. When the last dance started, a slow one, I pulled her close and nestled my face next to hers and held her tight whispering, "I am a bad time man. I am here for you and always will be now and in the future should you need me."

She whispered back, "This has been the best night of my whole life. Thank you for sharing it with me?"

There was a custom at prom called the kiss. When the last dance ended, the couples kissed and then walked two by two out the door.

The last dance ended. I pulled Jackie's chin up, took a deep breath, and then kissed her with the intention of not letting her go till we were the last ones left standing. It was really a big deal for me because I had never kissed a girl. I just concentrated on how they did it in the movies. I didn't want her to miss out on anything. When I released her grinning, the prom crowd was clapping for us; I could see tears in her eyes. She knew that I had sacrificed my reputation as a straight arrow for her and would be branded homosexual the following year.

She whispered, "If you need a prom date next year, I will fly back from California."

On my office desk today, sits a small framed prom photo of her in her stewardess outfit and me in the pilot one. We have been life time friends. I have taken her out to dinner numerous times and to many events that she has needed a male escort. A girl is a girl no matter what the costume body she wears. A man is a man no matter what costume body he wears. I have never forgotten the man modeling his wife's dress while she hemmed it. We are who we are on the inside. We are not the costume bodies we walk around in. Judge those about you by their inner person.

At Jackie's prom, I sacrificed my straight arrow ego to be there for her. I don't even remember the names of eighty percent of the kids we went to prom with that year. However, Jackie and I will not be forgotten. We were hot.

CHAPTER NINE

WEDDING BELLS

A week after prom, Jackie packed her bag and flew off to California to start a new life for herself; one of her choosing. Her parents gave her tuition and book money to start college there. I knew she intended to cash the check and enter cosmetology school instead. Jackie wanted to be a hair dresser to the stars. She had my thumbs up.

With Jackie gone, I was once more friendless and lonely. It had been a year and Jodi was still missing. There were missing person photos of Jodi posted everywhere. There were continuous whispers that the judge had somehow done away with her to keep her from testifying against him. I personally had received no contact from her. However, I felt inside that she was alive and well somewhere. We had spent so many nights together playing arcade games and talking that I was sure she had just walked away. She had spoken a couple of times about disappearing off of the face of the earth. Looking back, I now can see that she wanted to run away from something. I was just a fifteen year old kid at the time and didn't pick up on the fact she was stressed out. Apparently, she was infatuated with her uncle. She stayed up with me at nights because she was stressed from hiding her affair and unable to sleep. If I could go back, I would crawl thru her window every night and count to six till we both fell asleep. She needed me and I was just too immature to see it. I was there in her bad times, but I was a blind participant.

With June came a month long parade of weddings. The newspaper was always full of announcements and where the nuptials were to be held. I peeped at bride's hot feet and their weddings in the month of June. Some people call it being a wedding crasher. It is a form of peeping in on something private just like a window.

Reading the Sunday papers in late May, I made myself a list of thirty days of weddings. School was out and I was free to crash one each day for the month. It was a break from the night routine. I was starting to mature and the peeping in thru bathroom windows didn't hold the thrill it once had. I guess my peeping taste was maturing.

It was about the middle of June when I read about a biker couple that was getting married at a local little lower class wedding chapel. The chapel was an antiquated little store-front dive that had been remodeled and decorated like a tiny chapel. It was definitely an off the wall place to get married. The restrooms had posters hanging of the bride of Dracula and the bride of Frankenstein if that tells you anything. I checked the place out ahead of time just like I did houses holding night time parties. The chapel itself held about forty folding chairs and on the walls hung post-ers from different movies that were about weddings. Cheap fake flowers were everywhere and they probably had not been dusted or replaced in ten years. The place was tacky and catered to people wanting to quickly marry for some reason. On a scale of one to ten rating wedding chapels for class, it was a minus one or a two.

The biker couple's wedding was to be an afternoon affair with the reception to be held at a bar afterwards. I wasn't interested in the drunken reception afterwards. I got enough of drunks at home. However, I was sure the wedding would probably be interesting to watch. So, fifteen minutes before the wedding started, I entered on the heels of a family that had children. I sat down in the same row they did appearing to be with them. They ignored me. They had their hands full trying to control three kids that were elementary age and antsy. At the nicer weddings in the prominent churches across town, you didn't see children in attendance at weddings. Those weddings were invitations only and stated no children.

The chapel quickly filled up with adults and children. Some of the kids looked like they hadn't had their hair combed in three days. It was definitely a low class wedding and some of the attendees looked as bad as my mother and grandmother arriving in jeans and flip flops. I remained seated, although I was sure that I had made a mistake in crashing the low class event. I eyed all the women's feet and didn't see a decent pair of spikes on any of them. There were some biker women wearing black boots. However, even they looked hideous in their choice of apparel to wear to a wedding. They could have at least put on a pair of boots that had heels on them. They all looked like they were wearing men's boots.

I sat on my folding chair thinking the place was a little hot. Then I realized the back windows were up. The place had no air conditioning. Everyone in the place was going to be a sweat hog before the wedding was over. I could feel sweat trickling down the back of my neck. I looked at the eight or nine year old kid sitting next to me. His face was flushed red and you could see beads of perspiration on his nose. Maybe I was dreaming and I was sitting in Hell.

Perspiring from the extreme heat, I decided it was too late to escape. I was going to have to suffer thru the next hour. Wiping sweat from my brow, I made a mental decision to count tattoos on women. The men in attendance were covered with them. Women are little more squeamish with that sort of thing. I felt sure that the bride or her maids would not be openly displaying tattoos. The count would help me pass the time and the fact that the chapel was sweltering. I felt a drop of water run down the back of my neck.

The family sitting next to me started fanning themselves with pages the mother had just torn from a kid's book that she pulled from her big worn out sloppy handbag. She was even nice enough to tear out a page and hand it to me to fan with. I smiled at her and took it. I had to give her credit. She wasn't going to let her family suffer the heat if she could help it. That included destroying a kid's beginning reader book. She was a bad times woman and a survivor. Today, I would like to know who she was. That sheet of the storybook said she was a woman who cared. That storybook page is framed and hangs in my bedroom. I was really short in the department of someone caring about me back then.

(Storybook page woman, If you are out there somewhere, I think fondly and often about you. You are hot and definitely one of my treasured women.)

After a little fanning, the seven or eight year old boy sitting next to me asked, "Why are you 'thitting' with us?"

"I am afraid of the biker dudes! Your dad is big and I feel safe sitting with you." I whispered trying to appease the boy and not draw attention to myself.

"You are 'thmart'! My daddy is the bouncer at the Two 'Thots' Club. He can whoop any biker across the aisle. Where does your dad work?"

"My dad is a cook." I replied hearing some prelude music on a boom box starting. There would definitely not be any organ or harp played.

"Does he cook meth potatoes?" the kid asked.

I turned quickly and stared at him. He was too young to be asking something like that unless he had a problem like mine. Did his parents wrap rocks with foil and pass them off as baked potatoes on the grill?

"Yes," I replied to gain his trust. "Does yours?"

"My dad is too busy. My mom cooks the meth potatoes."

"Your mom cooks?" I replied questioning and glancing at the plump woman who had given me the story book page. She didn't look like the skinny hags that I knew that cooked meth. I couldn't fathom another kid going thru what I had.

"My name is Bump. What is yours?

"Billy . . . ," He replied. "I am a meth potatoes and gravy man."

I burst out in a snort. I realized that the kid had a speech impediment and he was referring to his mother making mashed potatoes and gravy. I was relieved.

"Right . . ." I said and then didn't say anything further. The wedding march music was starting.

I stood, turned, and faced the back like everyone else to watch the procession in of bride and attendants. I hadn't paid any attention to the groom and his best man up front because I had been busy with my brief conversation with Billy. I was amused. Perhaps the universe was sending me a new little friend named Billy to replace my Jackie who had flown away to a land called Hollywood. I would make a point of peeping at the Two Shots Club till I came up with an address for the bouncer family. I made up my mind to keep an eye on the kid even if he never saw me doing so. I needed someone to care for and think about. My life was pretty empty at the moment.

First down the aisle sauntered the traditional flower girl. She was carrying an Easter basket filled with fake rose petals which she was refusing to scatter. She had on tennis shoes with a fancy dress that I was sure had come from a thrift shop somewhere. There were visible stains down the front. Her hair was combed, but she had haunting black circles around her eyes. I wondered what had caused her gaunt look. She looked like a ragamuffin compared to the flower girls across town at the prominent church weddings. Standing there, I realized I was standing in low class wedding hell. Everyone in the building plus the wedding party was biker drunks and addicts who could have lived on my street and bought drugs from my parents. The flower girl probably was living a childhood nightmare just like the one that I was about to escape from. I never considered the fact that there were others out there like me.

Next down the aisle came the first bridesmaid. She had on scuffed up red platform shoes that were worn by cross dressers and stripper types. Her dress looked like something that she could jerk off in some sort of stripper frenzy. There were needle marks and tattoos running up her arms and she had made no effort in her dressing to conceal them. Instead of carrying flowers, she carried a bottle of cheap wine with a white bow tied around the neck. I was in shock. Her tattoos counted as number one.

Behind the first bride's maid, two more bridesmaids paraded in dressed equally as bad. One had on flip flops for shoes and the other was barefoot and drunk. There was no telling where the one had lost her shoes. The second and third bride's maids also had tattoos. My count was up to three. I just stood silently shaking my head. I was facing what my sister's life was going to be like as she slid down in the gutter further. I definitely did not want a life like I was seeing paraded.

Glancing up front, I could see the groom and his best man's eyes were extremely bloodshot. They were also both high. Who in their right mind takes wedding vows while too high to remember them? I found the affair quite disgusting. I glanced around the crowd and spotted a woman up front in shorts and a halter top controlling the boom box and cassette of wedding music. Her legs had snake tattoos running up the sides of her legs. She was number four. Who in the hell attends a wedding in a halter top and short shorts? As a rule, I didn't peep in the gutters of the city. This wedding was a surprise and I decided that I would definitely avoid the low class chapel in the future. I had four women with Tattoos. I needed two more and then I was out of there.

Just as I thought it couldn't get any worse, the bride stepped in the back door and prepared to walk down the aisle. One whole side of her face was tattooed as well as both shoulders and arms. I stood on my tip toes to get a look at her legs and feet. They were tattooed as well. She had on no nylons and there was visible crust and dirt on the sides of her feet. She wore yellowed white spikes that were at least forty years out of style. I couldn't believe it. She looked like a freak horror show doll in a teen fashion doll's white dress. In my thinking she had probably always wanted to get married in a strapless dress like some fashion doll she had played with when she was a kid. She wasn't the fashion doll type. What bride in their right mind would wear a strapless dress with all of her tattoos, flaws, and needle marks exposed? She definitely did not look feminine, loveable, or sexy. She looked trampy and could have given the bride of Frankenstein some serious competition. Her bleached blonde frizzy hair topped it all. It hadn't been washed or rolled before the wedding. It was just brushed back in a pony tail and at least an inch and a half of black uncolored roots was showing. Surely she looked in the mirror before she dressed. I recognized her veil as actually being a lace curtain panel with the hemmed ends cut off. I had seen a panel like it hanging in one of the houses I peeped in a few weeks before. I would in the future refer to her as the curtain veiled bride. I watched her as she took her place up front by the groom who was wearing jeans, a T-shirt, and a leather vest. He had on construction boots and a studded belt in his jeans. The bride was tattoo number five.

I scanned the crowd while the vows were being said. Too my utter surprise, I saw my mother sitting on the back row drunk as a skunk hanging on to the arm of some biker dude about my father's age. I quickly lowered my head and looked at my feet avoiding her. I wasn't sure when she had slipped in the back door to the wedding, possibly while I was eyeing the groom. Hopefully, she was too high to notice me. I did not know what she was doing at the wedding. There had been no mention at my house about a wedding. If her and the biker dude had a thing going, he had to be nuts.

My mother had nothing to offer except a ride down the drain of life. Alcohol and drugs had zapped her till she was a ninety pound, wrinkled, gaunt, wreck of a middle aged woman. Any man that would sleep with her had to be nuts because I knew she would sell herself occasionally for money to make drugs or buy alcohol. In my opinion, she was past the age and stage of anyone wanting her. I couldn't imagine the biker duded letting her hang on him. However, nothing surprised me with my family. Maybe my mother was having an affair.

At the moment, I just wanted to make an unnoticed exit so I wouldn't have to suffer the mouthy wrath of my mother. Life was never about me, but what her and my dad could get by with and not have law enforcement calling at our door. She wouldn't see the afternoon adventure with the biker dude as her doing something wrong. She would see it as me being a little snitch possibly following her. I was always watching my backside and staying out of my parent's way.

I spotted an emergency only exit door in the side of the building on my side. When the bride started to leave the chapel and all eyes were on her, I would slip thru that emergency exit. I knew my mother was up to something, but frankly, I didn't give a damn. When I graduated high school next year, I was going to catch a bus, go to California just like Jackie, and start a new life for myself and never look back. I planned to totally abandon my family just as they had me for a life time. I wanted to be somebody, have nice things, and be respected.

The ceremony ended and the bride and groom started to walk back down the aisle to exit. When they were half way down the center aisle and all eyes were on them, I hunkered down and walked to the emergency exit and quickly left setting off the alarm on the door. Outside, I ran like hell till I was blocks away from the chapel. I stopped in front of a bar and leaned against the outside of it to catch my breath. Then I realized that I had only counted five tattoos. That meant I had to have a sixth to complete my set. So, I turned around and walked back towards the wedding. I had to count six or I wouldn't be able to sleep later.

About half a block from the chapel, I saw that most of the crowd from the wedding had moved on probably to the bar reception. I walked up to the side of the chapel and peeped around to the front. I saw my mother sitting on the back of a bike hanging on to the biker dude and talking to a girl in jeans. I kept peeping till my mother left with the dude on the cycle. I breathed a sigh of relief and leaned on the side of the building thinking of an excuse to go back around front and eye the remaining women for tattoos. A teen girl walked around the corner. Seeing me, she smiled and leaned against the building with me. She had on jeans, boots, and biker's garb like the others who had attended the wedding. I recognized her as being one of the bridesmaids. She looked better in jeans that she did the crap dress she was wearing for the wedding.

"What is up with the woman and the dude on the bike you were talking to?" I asked striking up a conversation. "They don't exactly look like they could be a couple."

"The old hag makes meth. He buys from her. She has a crush on him and sells him drugs cheap. However, he laughs at her when she isn't around. He uses her and she is too much of an old dumb ass to see it."

"Was she invited to the wedding?" I asked trying to act casual about my question.

"No, she was delivering some drugs for the bridal couple to use tonight. They are a gift from the biker dude to the couple." She replied eyeing my ragged jeans.

"I see, a wedding present . . ."

"I, personally, am glad this piece of crap wedding is over." She said leaning and pulling a pack of cigarettes from her pocket and offering me one. "I hate weddings and women with no taste."

"I don't smoke." I replied and then added. "I like the way you look now in your jeans better than in that outdated hooker's dress you had on."

"That is what I told my mother. She insisted I wear that garage sale find. I didn't even want to be in the wedding, but was given no choice."

"Are you related to the bride?" I asked.

"She works with my mother out at the Two Shots Bar. The bride was trying to impress her respectable sister who was sitting in the back with a row full of kids. She needed a big wedding and bridesmaids. It didn't matter who the maids were. I got drafted. My mother owed her some sort of favor."

"So, the plump woman fanning herself wasn't one of you?"

"Nah . . . she drove in from out of state for the wedding.

She is divorced from the dude that was sitting with her. He is a bouncer out at the Two Shots Bar. I think this is his weekend to see his kids. Plump ass got religion a couple of years ago and left him. She wears a cross around her neck, walks the straight and narrow, and is possibly one of those door knockers who drive you crazy."

I fingered the story book page that I had folded and saved in my pocket. I was glad to know that the plump woman had chosen respectability. I would add the story book page to my important items that I kept stored in my locker at school.

"Where do you go to high school? I don't remember seeing you where I go." I asked wondering why she would tattoo herself and deface her body so young. In my book they made a girl look a little trampy or trashy.

"I quit school when I turned sixteen. I will always have a biker dude to look out for me. I won't need to work. Biker men want their women at home. Why bother wasting my time on books." She replied.

"What if the biker dude gets sick, you have a house full of kids, and you need to get a job to support yourself, him, and your family?"

"That will never happen to me. Charlie, my man, is a welder. He makes good money and I will be fine. I don't plan on having kids. He will buy me a trailer and we will live the good life. On weekends we will party and ride bikes."

I was shocked that her number one goal was to be kept by a man and settle for a mobile home somewhere. Her dreams were not very big.

About that time, a group of the last wedding attendees exited the building. I spotted a woman about the bride's age with a row of hearts running up one of her arms. That made six. I was okay to sleep for the night.

"What is your name?" I asked the girl. "My nickname is Bump."

"Tasha," she replied. "Why are you hanging around? Do you need a ride home?"

"No, I help clean up after everyone is gone." I replied lying. My tattered jeans made me look like a cleaning person. "I am just chilling out waiting."

"Oh . . . that makes sense. I never considered there were cute hunks that clean up after these affairs. Just so you know . . . I stuck my gum under the third chair's seat on row four. Chew it and think of me." She said walking away and winking at me.

I grinned at her and wondered how long her wink and her spirit would live. The drug, alcohol, and party scene killed the spark of those it captured sooner or later. I could picture her as my hag of a mother. She wouldn't be a pretty picture with time. She would be a walking Zombie.

I would stick with Jodi and Jackie. They had dreams of being someone. I wanted women in my life that were smart, educated, and looked good in spikes. I had lived a lifetime with a family of no respect and knew I definitely didn't want a future of that. Tasha's wink was a door opener to hell. I was smart enough not to take the door.

CHAPTER TEN

SURPRISE VISITOR

July and August crept by. Without Jackie, there wasn't much going on in my summer. When the weather was pretty, I slept on top of buildings or wherever I could find a quiet spot. I only went home if it was raining. Every day of summer was the same. I got an occasional letter from Jackie and she would tell me about her summer session of hair dresser classes. I dreamed of joining her in California. However, I was determined to graduate high school. In my mind, only low life dropped out of school. I wanted to be somebody. Jackie had graduated and she was becoming somebody. I didn't want her to be ashamed of me. She was all I had to cling to for a sense of sanity and belonging.

In July, I peeped for patriotic items. In August, I counted men who had hanging calendars with bikini supermodels on them. I wanted summer to end. During the school year, I was guaranteed one meal a day at lunch. I lost weight over summer due to my parents selling their food stamps for meth ingredients. I was eating out of fast food trash cans at night after the places closed. I was really tired of cold fries and whatever else customers pitched. Survival was a hard game that summer. I did manage to get on at the car wash mid-summer on Saturdays. The day's wages all went for food and what school supplies I would need for my senior year. I rented a bus locker downtown for the summer and that is where I kept what was important to me. Anything loose at my house got sold for alcohol or cigarettes. It was a struggle to keep the rent on my locker paid and my few things safe from my parents. It never occurred to me to go to summer school. When you live with uncaring parents you never get any direction or suggestions for doing well in school or otherwise. They are more likely to give you a fix and put you to watching the meth or the driveway for cops. Making a decision to work the one day at the car wash and using the money to rent myself a bus locker to keep my things safe was a major financial plan for me at seventeen. I didn't have a driver license yet and the thought of owning a car was a fantasy. After paying my bus locker rental fee each week, I had nine dollars left to eat on for a week plus buy my school supplies. At that point in my life, macaroni and cheese wasn't even an option for me. My parents had sold the kitchen stove for money to guy the ingredients to make a batch of meth. There was no way to cook and I had no friends to drop in on for a meal or to use their stove.

Jodi was still missing and posters of her were plastered around the city. She had been gone for about fourteen or so months. It had also been that long since I ceased meeting Granny Snoop. I was really lonely and extremely happy when classes of my senior year started the last week in August. The car wash had an equipment failure and closed down in early September. I was once more living basically out of my school locker and eating one meal a day in the school cafeteria that I did dishes for. My parents wouldn't sign the paperwork for me to participate in the free lunch program for poor kids. They thought it would bring social workers to their door and they were all about avoiding cops and social workers. Whether I ate or not didn't matter to them. My student counselor secured the one hour position in the cafeteria as a dishwasher for me. When you are a teen, it is embarrassing to have your friends seeing you do dishes for your lunch. I appreciated my school lunch but also suffered ridicule from the jocks and cheer leaders for it. I was bottom of the barrel in the social ranking of my senior class. I kept telling myself that I was almost home free. When I got my diploma, things were going to change for me.

In September of my senior year, I was called to the office. I had a visitor. The principal showed me into a school conference room. I was shocked to see Granny Snoop sitting there at a table waiting for me. She looked ill behind her gold rimmed glasses. On the table in front of her was an unopened brief case. I took a seat across from her not knowing what to say.

"You look surprised to see me," she stated waving the principal out.

"No more surprised than I was to find out that you were a shrink and not a peeper. You lied to me about living in an old person's apartment building and being a peeper. You and Jodi both lied to me." I spouted."

"I wasn't up front with you. You are right about that." She stated eyeing me. "My name is Doctor Jones."

"Why are you here, Granny Snoop or should I call you Doctor Jones?"

"I am a psychiatrist, Bump, and have dedicated my life to helping kids in bad situations. I saw a chance to help you when I found you at the window that night. I am sorry that I have let you down, I do care about you. I have actually missed our window meetings."

"Well, if it makes any difference to you, I still count and pray for you on Mondays." I replied eyeing her."The Big Smoke Man can't help it because you are deceitful. He just deals with cigarette habits. Maybe I will have to consult the Big Man of Lies to deal with your deceit."

Granny Snoop broke out in a grin. "I am down to just one or two cigarettes a day. You and the Big Smoke Man have a right to be proud of me on that count."

"Why are you here, Granny? I am not fifteen anymore and looking for someone, anyone, to love me. I am seventeen and planning to move to California in a few months when my senior year is over. What do you want from me?"

"It has come to my attention from the clerk at the convenience store that you were friends with my granddaughter Jodie. I honestly didn't know that she was sneaking out and hanging out with you at night. She kept her friendship with you a guarded secret from me for some reason."

"I have given my friendship with Jodi a lot of thought. She couldn't date the old dude she wanted to be with, so she hung with me six nights a week to keep from stressing out. I was like a tranquilizer of some sort to her and she didn't want you to know about me. I think she was afraid you would take me from her. I can see now that you would have. You didn't want me at your house. I seem to remember you lying to me and telling me you lived in a Hi-rise."

"I am desperate, Bump, to find Jodi. Do you know where she is or have you heard from her? Worse yet, do you know from the underbelly of the city what might have happened to her."

"Why do you want to find her?"

"To apologize to her and try to start over. I love her."

"You and I are in the same boat. I told her I disliked her prom dress and she wasn't speaking to me the night she disappeared."

"Did she talk about seeing anyone other than you and the judge?"

"She went to the prom with the jeep driving dude, but dumped him after she got there. I was at the prom with my friend Jackie. We were shaking a lot of cars acting stupid scaring prom couples. I was totally shocked when the old fart you got arrested exited a red compact madder than hell with Jodi also doing the same."

"Do you know who the old dude was?" She asked surprised.

I was peeping after the prom and just happened to walk upon your little side show on his lawn. One of his neighbors in the crowd of spectators told me all about you, the judge and Jodi."

"I was shocked to find that you weren't who you said you were. I read all about you, your brother the judge, and Jodi the next morning in the newspaper."

"Do you think it was possible that Jodi was a call girl?" She asked with a sad look in her eyes.

"No, I think she thought she was in love with the old

dude. She couldn't come to you because she was related to him. My friend Jackie thinks she might have seen in him something missing, a father figure maybe."

'"The night I met you, I was looking thru my medicine cabinet trying to find something for a headache and discovered birth control pills. I thought they possibly belonged to one of my overnight guests that were there for the party. The judge is my brother and I have denied rumors about him for years. I have been blind thinking him respectable and not capable of being a pervert. After Jodi left with her date for the prom, I settled in my office to do some paperwork. About midnight, I took a really bad headache after speaking on the phone with some old woman who was insisting that my brother was sleeping with Jodi. The headache was probably caused by my blood pressure sky rocketing. I didn't believe the voice on the phone and drove over to my brother's house to tell him about the phone call. Judges get a lot of threats from people they have sentenced. I just wanted to make sure that he was okay. I let myself in because he wears a hearing aid. When he doesn't have it on, he can't hear the doorbell. I let myself in with my key and made my way back to his bedroom and walked in on him and Jodi. I had him arrested for incest and sleeping with a minor. When they released Jodi the next morning after questioning and a night in juvenile hall, she was to return to school. I left money for her to go by taxi. I had a full schedule the next morning and to be truthful I was very angry with her and just needed a little space to collect myself before confronting her about the situation. I didn't want to say things that I would regret. She didn't make it to school. She just disappeared."

"My friend Jackie is gay. She thinks Jodi is different and

prefers older men just like she prefers partners that are not the norm. She sees Jodi as being born unusual like her, just in different way."

"So you think Jodi preferred older men and she was afraid to tell me about it?"

"Falling for your brother probably was not planned. My friend Jackie thinks Jodi was afraid you would abandon her like you did her father if you discovered she was attracted to older men." I stated unsmiling and studying her face. I then added. "She thinks you abandoned her father because he owed you money, or some simple thing. Her and your brother was not a simple thing and she was stressed you were going to throw her out and not love her anymore."

"Oh shit . . ." Granny Snoop stated. "You better pray hard for me next Monday night. I feel a two carton cigarette mental break down coming on. I never guessed she had a thing for older men. I can also see where her perception of my abandoning her father has pushed her over the edge."

"I was blind back then, Granny Snoop. However, I can see now why she couldn't sleep at night and needed me to hang on to. Jodi was walking a tightrope with you."

"My son, Jodi's father, started out as a peeping Tom like you and then entered the night world of criminal activity, drugs, and alcohol. Jodi was born to him and a street prostitute. I sued for custody of Jodi and the courts awarded her to me. She had cigarette burns all over her, head lice, and hadn't been fed in days. I had the choice of abandoning my son and being awarded Jodi, or hanging on to my son and watching him take Jodi down the drain of life."

"So that is the big secret that Jodi doesn't know? Her dad

is an alcoholic and a drug dealer?"

"I have tried to protect her from him. My son lives across the city in a dump where he deals in anything and every-thing that is illegal. He and his second wife live in squa-lor along with her two kids and a woman they say is her mother. I haven't spoken to or seen them since the day I got custody of Jodi. Do you know how I can find Jodi?"

"I honestly have not heard from her. What is your son's name?" I asked alarmed that her son and family sounded like mine.

"His name is Barnard Jones." She replied.

I was in shock. Barney Jones across the tracks was my step -father. I tried not to react. "Have you ever met your son's second wife and her two kids?" I asked.

"I saw her in the courthouse when I was fighting for cus-tody of Jodi. She had a twelve year old girl with her and a little boy toddler age. I think my son married her because he was trying to prove to the court that he had a home, a wife, and a stable home for Jackie. I hired detectives to prove that she was an unfit mother as well as a prostitute. She actually caused my son to lose Jodi. Marrying her was a big mistake on his part. I produced photos of his new wife working the streets. She had a history of child abuse, had aborted four babies, and had three children that were taken away from her prior to the birth of the twelve year old girl. My detective had photos of her two children being filthy, neglected, and playing unsupervised in the streets. It was a hard choice, but I chose to abandon my son and give Jodi a stable home."

"Wasn't the little boy worth rescuing like your granddaughter?"

"I took what was mine, Bump. That was all that I could legally do."

"What is family made up of, Granny Snoop? Isn't it more than blood? I know a couple of kids at school that are adopted and they have good families and lives. Wouldn't it have been an act of love on your part to have seen that the other two kids were adopted out or something?"

"It is all hind sight, Bump. I rescued one child. It was a fight in the courts to do that. The two children by my son's second wife had grandparents. They should have stepped up to the plate."

"At school they talk about no child left behind. You left behind two children that could have been family to you."

"I did what I felt I needed to do. Do you have any clue as to where I can find Jodi? I want to make things right with her."

"I haven't heard from Jodi. However, I am a kid that peeped into your window and learned to love you. I didn't know who you were back then or now till this moment. You were Granny Snoop and I was Bump. I am your son Barney's second wife's son. I don't carry your son, Barney's last name of Jones. My older sister and I have lived in hell with no one to love us or care whether we lived or died. For some unknown reason, fate let Jodi and I meet. She is everything to me. I would walk thru hell and back for her. Fate also let me fall in love with you. I wish it had been a two way street and not just a mind game with you. It has been fourteen months since I saw you last. You have sent no detectives looking for me."

"Oh shit . . ." she said the blood draining from her face. "I didn't see this one coming."

"I am just a kid who has had to survive a bad set of parents that you could have rescued me from. I was a second Jodi burnt with cigarettes, beat, and starved. Your wanting to help kids is a bunch of crap in my book. I needed rescued but there was no one there for me or my sister." I stated with tears in my eyes, got up, and started to walk out.

"Wait, Bump. I honestly didn't know all of these months that you were Barnard's step son. Please talk with me about Jodi. You don't want her turning out like your dad do you? Help me find her, please."

"I have not heard from her. She is just as lost to me as she is to you."

"I don't know what to say. Please, Bump, help me for Jodi's sake. I was playing a mind game with you at the windows. I wanted to help you. I did get you to stay home one night and saying prayers for me instead of peeping. I saw that as a minor success. In the back of my mind I was trying to point you away from a life of future crime. I saw my son Barnard in you."

"I don't need you, Granny Snoop. I am going to be someone. I am surviving and doing what I have to till I get my hands on my diploma. I have no intentions of being a degenerate piece of crap like your son who has beat me, starved me, and made me live in filth. I am not a gutter rat. I may live in the gutter with your son, but not for much longer. I have plans."

"Just tell me if you think Jodi was a hooker before she left so I will know how to help her when I find her. She won't be coming home a child."

"I honestly don't know if Jodi was a hooker back then. She told me she worked at the lumberyard till ten every night except Saturday and Sunday. She had lots of money to spend on Arcade games. I never saw her before ten-thirty at night. What she did between the time school let out and ten I don't know. She told me she worked at the lumber yard. I never went out there. I never had a reason to. Only you know whether she worked out there or not. Answer the question for yourself. I don't want to know. I want to remember Jodi as my friend and the only girl I will ever truly love."

"I see . . . The lumber yard." She replied and then didn't say anymore. Her face said it all.

"Jodi was walking a mental tight rope with you. She has a screw loose just like me. You loosened hers by not letting her know her father and my parents loosened mine. Jodi felt her loose screw would cause you to abandon her. She couldn't handle the prospect. I keep trying to turn my screw and tighten it. One day I will escape your son and my mother. I could have escaped as a child if you had taken the time to care about the other two children who didn't have your blood in them. Jodi has escaped the tight-rope here and is trying to tighten her screw in my opinion."

"I have been an idiot. I want you now, Bump. For one thing, you have a connection with the Great Smoke Man and I haven't been totally cured of my habit yet."

I turned amused. She had a way of getting to me. How do you stop loving someone? I wanted to tell her to go to hell, at the same time I was a sponge wanting what we once had!

"Damn you, Granny Snoop, you have a screw loose as bad as mine. Meet me at midnight at the convenience store arcade and I will walk you thru what Jodi and I used to do at night. Maybe you can pick up on something that I have been to blind to see. I honestly don't know where she is." I said turning to walk out.

"I will be there. What do you want me to wear?"

I turned back and grinned at her. "Granny clothes of course! Have a twenty on you for the games. Jodi always beat the pants off of me. I will see if you have her blood in you."

She stretched her arms out to me. I couldn't resist them or her. All my life I had wanted to be held and loved. I walked over to her, hugged her, and then walked out and returned to classes.

Granny Snoop and I spent one wild night walking in Jodi's shoes. I even took her out to where I had first met her when she climbed out of the lumber yard truck. Two days later, Granny Snoop had a heart attack and died. I attended her funeral and wept for the grandmother that wasn't really mine. I never told my father about my relationship with her. I didn't want her memory destroyed by his hatred for her.

After Granny Snoop reentered my life, I started to separate myself from my father and start to refer to him as my stepfather. I think it was part of starting to sprout adult wings. I was ready to leave the nest and him. I was letting go of him and the home I no longer desired to be a part of.

CHAPTER ELEVEN

THE OBITUARY

I wanted to keep my relationship with Granny Snoop a secret. However, I did feel my stepfather deserved to know that his mother had passed away. I purposely left a newspaper open on the kitchen table to the obituary page. The family thought my sister had purchased it and left it behind. She had moved out that morning and in with a guy she had met at a bar. Down deep, I wanted to hear my stepfather's side of the story. Surprisingly, there was no reaction from him when my grandmother discovered the obituary notice and handed it to him to read. He just got up from the table and went about his day. I did hear my maternal grandmother make a remark to my mother, "The bitch is dead. Barnard should inherit everything. You should leave him as soon as you get your hand on some of that money and get me and you out of this dump." Nothing more was said.

I did not want any of my family knowing I knew Granny Snoop for fear of repercussions. I still feared being beat by my dad. Worse would be my mother's mouth thinking I had somehow betrayed her. To be honest, I would have walked out on my stepfather, maternal grandmother, sister, and mother in a heartbeat if Granny had ever asked me to live with her. She didn't. I like to think that she would have eventually.

I attended the funeral and sat in seclusion in the rear in case my parents showed up. They did not. Only I grieved her death along with a roomful of friends and work associates. She was definitely respectable. Even the judge, her brother, made an appearance sucking it up. My stepfather should have sucked it up.

On Monday following the funeral, my stepfather and mother contacted the attorney for Granny Snoop's estate thinking they were going to inherit her big house and everything due to Jodi's disappearance. A reading of the will was scheduled and I and my parents sat in Granny Snoop's attorney's office. To their surprise, Granny Snoop had signed her big house and insurance policies over before she died to the local children's home. In the will she left Barnard Jones one dollar, his wife one dollar, and her two children one dollar each. The children's home got everything except the dollar bills. In her will she presumed Jodi to be dead and left her nothing.

The big surprise at the reading of the will came in the form of a brown cardboard box which had been retrieved from a bank storage vault by the attorney. In her will, she stated the box was to become the property of the district attorney to help rid the city of its scum as well as possibly finger the person causing Jodi Jones and couple of other girls to disappear. She listed my father as the possible murderer of Jodi due to greed over her estate. She told of how my stepfather killed dogs and cats when he was young and walked down a spiral path into a life as a sociopath. The box contained old newspaper clippings and a small collection of souvenirs that didn't make sense in my eyes, but were supposedly taken by my father from crime scenes when he lived at home. In the box was an odd collection of junk jewelry, cigarette lighters, and women's underwear. I quickly stood and peeped trying to get a closer look at what was in the box. The lawyer took the top off and briefly held the box and contents up for those sitting to have a brief look but wouldn't let anyone touch them. In shock, my father rose with a face white as a sheet and backed out of the room with my mother in tow thinking they might be arrested on the spot. My parents drug me along to the reading of the will thinking somehow I was inheriting part of the estate as a step grandson. However, in their frenzy to leave, they forgot I even existed and left me sitting. I had to walk home when it was over. The district attorney sitting at the reading of the will left quickly after the reading taking the box with him. He was all smiles.

I sat in on the reading of the will because Granny Snoop had left me and my sister one dollar. I think she wanted me to hear how really perverted my parents were! I already knew how twisted mean, and uncaring my parents were. I had lived a life in their world of perversion. I respected Granny Snoop. In the end, she stood for respectability and doing what was right. She definitely was not a bitch as my maternal grandmother called her when I got home. My maternal grandmother, on the other hand, could wear the title well.

The rest of September and October were crazy around my house. I heard my parents whispering that they needed to make one last big batch of drugs in order to have money to run on. There was no doubt in their mind that they were going to be eventually arrested for some of the crimes as soon as evidence was collected. For the first time in years, they were fairly sober and one of them always stood guard at the front window in case they needed to make a run for it. They kept their old beat up car parked across the alley in a burnt out house's driveway in case the police blocked the alley. They were constantly watching the street and alley for police cars. They were also waiting for my grandmother's social security check to come in so they could buy ingredients for their last batch. The food stamp card came in first and as usual, they sold it leaving those in the house including me with nothing to eat. My school lunch was my main food source. I was surviving on one meal at school plus what I could scrounge from fast food trash cans. I had no family or friends that I could drop in on for a meal or a clean place to sleep. The old man that I mowed grass for went into a nursing home over the summer. Looking back, I wish I had spent more time with him. I didn't realize he was my friend till Jackie's prom. Young people are stupid in thinking that friends have to be their age. I could have had a safe house with him had I not been so young and blind. So what if he kept ten dogs and six cats in the house. None of us are perfect.

My maternal grandmother stayed half sober now fearing she was going to be arrested. My parents secretly intended to take her check, make a batch of drugs, sell them, and then leave her behind. I tuned in on their whispers one afternoon as they were standing out by the barbecue grill wrapping rocks in foil to look like baking potatoes. My maternal grandmother was a naive drunken dumbass. They planned to take me along because they needed me to beg charity for. They were users of me and anyone else they could turn for a dollar. I wasn't going with them. They just didn't know it. Long ago, I had started stashing what was important to me in my school locker and in a bus station locker in the summer. My birth certificate, special class notes thrown at me from Jodi and Jackie, one storybook page, a copy of Granny Snoop's will, and photos of Granny Snoop and Jodi were amongst the locker stored items. After the reading of the will, I moved my pillow, quilt, two sets of clothes, and the pilot and stewardess outfits to the top of the charred burnt out residence on fifth. No one went up there. I didn't have much, but I wanted those items when I started my new life after high school. I was not going with my parents. I would eat at school, scrounge food from trash cans at night, and bathe in the school's gym showers. I was finishing high school; to hell with my parents. When they fled, I would take up residence in the top of the charred burnt house. I was already staying away from home as much as possible and sleeping wherever I could find a dry spot.

I did my thing after the day of the reading of the will and ignored my parents who were half sober and scrounging for every dollar they could get a hold of. It was a time of grief for me. I had never had anyone love me, and the few times Granny Snoop had physically hugged me haunted me. I just couldn't let her go. I returned over and over to the funeral home peeping thru windows and attending stranger's funerals trying to get a grip on losing her.

On a rainy evening the middle of October, a wake for a stranger was scheduled. I slipped in when the funeral home director wasn't looking and hid in the little music and minister's alcove to one side of the chapel. Funerals and wakes had become my focus as I grieved. Each night I would attend a different one and set my usual goal of six things to look for so I could sleep. I just had to be inside that funeral home where I last said my goodbye to Granny Snoop. I had a screw loose that I couldn't tighten. Obsessive grief can be a loose screw.

One strange phenomena that I discovered during my weeks of wake and funeral peeping was how many casket peepers there are. After the first night or two of attending wakes or family nights, I started to pick them out of the crowds. They like me attended nightly. I wondered if they had to peep to sleep like me. I kept my distance from them and hid in the tiny alcove nightly peeping and listening. There was a small storage closet back there behind curtains that I could step into to hide if necessary filled with flower racks. No one saw me or questioned me. Years of peeping had made me good at what I did.

There was a lighter side to wake and funeral peeping. People viewing the dead say the craziest things. On this particular night, I had made a dart for my alcove to hide not having time to take a quick look at the deceased in the casket. I was sure it was a man. I could see a suited arm from where I was hidden. I decided to count odd things the wake attendees said to the body in the casket.

That night was my fifteenth or sixteenth wake. I was sitting behind the piano in the shadows watching a few people filter in and out looking at the deceased whoever he was. I didn't know him, so a name was of no importance to me. I could see the corpse's one blue suited arm. I was there to grieve Granny, not him.

There didn't seem to be any relatives sitting and crying on the front row as they usually did at wakes. So, I didn't have to be too careful about staying hidden. I sat on the piano bench in the secluded alcove and watched as two younger women in their thirties entered the chapel. They looked like secretaries or office workers. They made their way to the casket and casually peeped in snickering. They quickly look around to make sure they weren't being heard. There was no one in the chapel and they could not see me as I sat in dark seclusion. One nudged the other, snickered, and started a conversation.

"The old fart won't be pulling any fast ones now." The taller of the two said.

"Jones snipped his pulling chain." The other stated and then snickered.

"Pulling chain . . .," the other one laughed. "I have never heard it called that before."

My ears perked up. Were they referring to Granny and the judge? I craned my neck and stood on my tip toes to try to get a look at the dead man in the casket. What I could mostly see were his clothes and prune like, shrunken white hands that were folded across him. I watched as the pair of women sat down on the front row for a few moments to pretend to grieve. I counted their conversation as number one odd thing said at the wake for the evening. I also decided that they must not have respected the old dude too much. I would take a closer look at him when the viewing chapel was empty of visitors.

Next an old woman about seventy came in wearing a black dress accompanied by a young dude wearing jeans and a college logo sweatshirt. The guy seemed totally uninterested as though he had just possibly driven her to the wake or something. He sat down on the back row and pulled a cell phone from his pocket and appeared to be texting with someone, probably a friend. I liked the hooded college sweat shirt he had on. Someday I was going to have nice things to wear. I was just about there.

The elderly woman slowly made her way down front limping and holding onto a cane. I guessed she had probably been in a car wreck once upon a time and had a bad leg from it. She was respectable looking and perfectly dressed in black attire. Her hair was done as well as her nails. I glanced at her feet. She had on sensible shoes with short heels and black hose. For an old woman I liked her feet. They were respectful feet. If I was seventy, I would want my woman to have respectful feet at a funeral. Only sluts wore sling backs and open toes to funerals. I had figured that out from my ten or so nights of funeral and wake viewings. I am a peeper. I know street walkers when I see them. I also know a respectable woman when I see her.

"I watched as she put her nicely manicured old hand on top of the corpse's for a moment. Then she pulled it back and leaned in to him whispering. "Your days as a pervert are over. May you rot in Hell for all the emotional misery and shame you have dumped on me, your children, and sister?" Then she pulled a white hankie from her black respectable purse and dabbed her eyes. After a few minutes she left and the two secretary types left right behind her.

I was a little in shock. Apparently, the woman in black was the dude's wife or ex- wife. Having a light bulb turning on moment, I wondered if the dude in the casket was Jodi's Judge. The elderly lady's words counted as number two in my quest for odd things said to a corpse for the night.

I stayed in seclusion because a small handful of individuals entered and made their way up and circled the front of the casket. I could see that a couple of them were police officers. Three were girls I recognized as seniors from my freshman year of high school. They had to be nineteen or twenty now. I listened. No one was crying and the girls looked like they were a bit frightened of the man in the casket. Then one of the police officers asked lowly.

"This is your last chance to tell. He can't hurt you. He is dead." One of the policeman stated leaning in and whispering to the group.

I couldn't hear the girl's replies. They had their backs to me and they were whispering. I wondered what was so important that two policemen would bring three young women to view a corpse. The old dude and his visitors definitely had my attention. I now had three odd remarks.

After the policemen and girls left, a black man in his forties entered wearing a chauffeur's hat and uniform. I watched him make his way forward and stand in front of the casket. He then looked around to see if anyone was watching. Seeing he was alone, I watched him quickly spit into the face of the corpse and then grin from ear to ear.

"That is for all the times you looked down on me. Now it is me looking down on you and may you rot in Hell." He then turned and walked out before anyone else entered.

That was odd saying number four. I wondered whose chauffeur he was. The judge drove a red four door compact. I decided the chauffeur had to work for one of the judge's lady friends or possibly for his ex- wife who was possibly rich.

A couple of guys entered next in their late twenties. Both wore nice business suits. You could tell they were twin brothers. They walked up to the casket and just quietly stared for a few moments. They didn't show any signs of grief. They weren't crying or making sad faces. They stood with their hands behind their backs in silence. I thought they were going to stand like that for ever. I was getting antsy. Finally one of them spoke.

"It looks like someone has spit in his face. He is our dad. Do we wipe it off?"

The other one replied, "No, mom probably did it. Just leave it. She is paying for the funeral. If she wants spit on his face, he is going down that way."

They didn't stay after their discussion about the spit. Their words were odd saying number five. I had one to go and I could sleep for the night.

I continued to watch different ones come and go. Many of them I knew from peeping thru their windows. I kept listening but wasn't hearing anything else too off the wall being said. Just as I was about to give it up for the night and slip out the back door of the musician's alcove, I saw a familiar face enter the chapel door and make her way to stand in front of the casket. I recognized my maternal grandmother and she was half sober for once in her life. Surprisingly, she was showered and had her hair curled. That was a first. I watched the chapel door expecting my mother to walk thru. She accompanied my grandmother. My grandmother wasn't too steady on her feet at times. I didn't spot my mother anywhere. I watched and listened. She walked up to the casket and put her trembling hand on top of the old dude's and left it there as she leaned in and spoke.

"Well, Mack, you thought it was funny asking me a poor girl to the prom and then standing me up. I may have been a fool then, but you are the fool now. I tipped the police off about your sleeping with your niece. I have been keeping track of you for forty years or so. I knew one day I would catch you with an under aged girl and get even with you. Prom night is the only night I stay sober every year. I stood in the shadows at Barney's girl's prom and saw my grandson rock your red compact. I was surprised when I saw you and Barney's girl jump out half naked. I called your sister. Revenge is sweet and your reputation is zilch. It has taken me a lot of years to find a way to get even. You will be lowered in your grave as a man of disrespect, a child molester. You are a coward hanging yourself and taking the easy way out."

"Oh shit . . ." I muttered and then slapped my hand over my mouth and ducked out the back door of the musician's room and then out the back door of the mortuary and ran. I didn't like my maternal grandmother, but I wouldn't interfere or tell about her moment of revenge. She was the voice on the phone to Granny Snoop tipping her off. My maternal grandmother's words were odd saying number six.

Funerals are notorious for people saying phrases like, "He looks so natural, they did a good job on him, or why doesn't he have his glasses on?" I heard them all during the weeks I was peeping and grieving for Granny Snoop. The glasses remark always baffled me. Who sleeps with their glasses on? You would be surprised how many people are buried with their glasses on. Families want them to see down there in the dark, I guess. Also puzzling to me, is why everyone is buried in their dress clothes. I don't sleep in a business suit. I sleep in my boxers or ala natural. Wouldn't it make more sense to sleep for eternity in pajamas or your birthday suit? Also, let's face it, no one looks natural with their mouth sewn shut, their face drained of color, and funeral parlor white face powder brushed all over them. Natural for me now is a four o'clock shadow, boxers to sleep in, and a smile on my face from thinking about the women in my life. I have yet to see a corpse smile, sleep for eternity in his boxers, or have a four-o'clock shadow.

Maybe I will insist that the funeral home man sew my mouth shut at death in a smile, doing a little nip and tuck here and there. I am lucky. I have had a life time full of women with gorgeous feet to smile about. Jodi was the first. Granny Snoop and Jackie came after her. The women that came later are for another story and another day. I am a foot man.

CHAPTER TWELVE

CARMEN THE HIGH FLYER

It was Halloween and I hadn't left my house yet for an evening of peeping. My parents had their front porch light off. They didn't waste money on foolishness like giving away candy. I sat awhile at the front window watching mothers with toddlers making the round of the neighborhood trick-or- treating just before dark. There were numerous Halloween parties around town. However, I like most poor kids with family white trash reputations, wasn't invited to any of them. It was no secret around town that my parents were drunks and drug dealers. At fifteen, I thought I was keeping it hidden. By seventeen, you know that there are certain things that can't be hidden.

Looking thru our front window where the curtains were hanging half off a sagging, broken rod, I watched children that were fright night delighted, well cared for, and had on purchased Halloween costumes which to me was a sign of being okay financially. During my childhood, I wandered out into the festive night as some cheap, painted face Zombie wearing an old white T-shirt. I knew even when I was a kid that my parents always gave me the short end of the stick in everything. Even my bag of candy was taken from me when I got home. My parents and maternal grandmother ate it up with me getting four or five pieces. They saw it as breakfast for the next week. When I got up about the fourth grade, I got smart and put myself a sack out back and dumped my choice candy, the candy bars and apples in it before entering the house with my Halloween loot. We never had fruit at our house. Eyeing the little kids make their rounds trick-or-treating only made me sad for the childhood that had been stolen from me.

The treat at our house for Halloween, according to my father, was the batch of meth they were cooking out back which was going to buy the three of us a bus ticket to a new life. I just listened to him rattle on. He was already half drunk for the night. I wasn't going anywhere with him or my mother. They just didn't know it. Mom sold the month's food stamps for meth ingredients and my maternal grandmother threw her small social security pension in on the fund not realizing that they planned to dump her. She was looking forward to starting over somewhere far, far away.

You would have thought that my parents lived well on selling and making drugs. Not so, they were addicts and had to feed their own habits. They sold just enough to make the next new batch and keep the rest for themselves. I lived with three nut cases who most of the time did not know that I was a child that needed food or clothing. I was like a mouse that ran in and out a hole in the floor with them ignoring me.

It was Halloween and the meth was cooking. My parents had the foil covered rocks on the grill with the cologne spiked bottle of sweet barbecue sauce setting next to them. Four canned dog food meat patties sat waiting on a plate on the kitchen cabinet to throw on the grill should cops show up. There was no need in their mind of wasting meth money on real hamburger. It was just something to slap on the grill and throw sweet barbecue sauce on if the cops came to inquire what the odors and fumes were coming from our place. Social Workers were the most common to call on us. A couple of months prior, my mother convinced a restaurant to buy twelve huge cans of coffee with her food stamp card and then pay her a third of the cost in cash. That purchase was questionable and my mother told the worker that she had decided to store a year of coffee because she had got it on sale. When the worker asked to see it, my mother went into her fainting I am having a heart attack act. An ambulance came for my mother who could roll her eyes back in her head at will. The coffee incident was forgotten and slipped thru a crack somewhere.

It was about six-thirty in the evening. My father was drunk and cooking meth in the garage. My mother was playing front window guard, keeping an eye out for cops. My maternal grandmother had a bottle of cheap wine and was sitting at the kitchen table tying one on early. Also sitting at the table was my sister with her head face down on her folded arms. She had moved back in again. Her live in stint with the bar guy lasted four days. She stole money from his wallet and he beat her to a pulp. She just couldn't stay out of my parent's gutter. In one hand, she held a half empty vodka bottle and was about to drop it. I saw no reason to stay home. Eventually, the drunks in my house would get violent, mouthy, and possibly make me their punching bag. By midnight they would be passed out or so high you couldn't get them and their mouths off of the ceiling. I was fed up with my family and just chomping at the bit to sprout wings and fly. However, I was hanging in there for graduation. To me, my diploma was my first step to respectability and I wanted that desperately. I wanted what was behind the windows I peeped in.

My plan for the evening was to peep thru windows at different Halloween parties that were going on around town. I had met Jackie that way. We peeped in at prom. I really missed her companionship. I wanted a friend so bad that I could taste it. I was so lonely. Jackie had been gone for about five months and from her letters seemed happy in her new life in California. I was happy for her.

Ignoring my drunken grandmother and my sister at the table, I took a quick glance at my mother seated by the front window as a guard for the evening. She looked like death warmed over. She weighed all of ninety pounds and her lack of concern for her body read old hag. Her hair hadn't been cut or trimmed in at least five years. It was graying and she had really black raccoon eyes. She looked pitiful. However, I could not feel sorry for her. Drugs and alcohol had done it to her. She had chosen both.

"Bye Mom! Happy Halloween! " I half yelled wanting her to acknowledge me and the fact that it was a special night for kids.

"Get lost asshole. I am busy. Go play with yourself or something." She replied in a calloused voice.

Her words hurt. I was sure that a respectful mother would not say something like that to a son. If I had a son, I definitely wouldn't want her to say those words to him.

Just as I was about to exit the back door on the lean-to porch, my dad walked in with a little cigar hanging from his lip. He was getting really careless. I knew he was cooking, smoking, and drinking which was a bad combination. My gut feeling was that I needed to find someplace safe to sleep for the night. I hated the sick sweetening smell of the drugs cooking. I was seventeen and not too frightened of him anymore. I had a growing spurt over the summer and I was half a head taller than him. The slapping or punching me days were over.

"Dad, you really shouldn't be smoking that cigar, drinking, and cooking at the same time. Tonight could be an unlucky night!" I stated in disgust.

"When you can cook and bring in the dough, then give me your opinion you little bastard." He said pushing past me and yelling to my mother. "Get out the burgers, Trudy. The police are at the end of the block watching the kids. They may be watching us." He then grabbed the opened Vodka bottle from my sister's hand, turned it up and drank the last inch or so that was left in it. He looked frightened.

I watched as my mother flew in her half drunken stat e to the kitchen counter and removed the paper plate with the rings of dog food on it and head for the grill pushing past me. The spatula and bottle of cologne spiked barbecue sauce was already out by the grill along with the aluminum wrapped rocks to pass off as potatoes. I threw up my hands, grabbed my parka with a hood, and headed out the back door.

My parents alcohol and drug induced mad lifestyle was about to get the best of me. If it wasn't for winter coming on, I would have moved out and lived on top of the fast food restaurant till graduation. However, that wasn't possible in the winter months. I needed to survive November, December, January, February, and March. April and May

I could survive living on a roof top or beneath an overpass somewhere till I made it thru graduation. I just had to survive and that meant sucking it up and sleeping wherever I could on the nights home was intolerable.

I glanced one more time at my grandmother and sister who were passed out on the kitchen table shaking my head and left. Down deep, I secretly wished my family would blow themselves up with their cooking of meth and end my life of misery. I really didn't think I had any feelings for them. They had never shown me any form of love and respect. I wanted to be free from them. Love and respect to me was what I looked at thru windows; mothers rocking babies and dads helping kids with homework.

Walking out the back door, I considered what my theme for peeping would be for the night. I was getting older and had just about looked for everything imaginable. Lately, the counting to six to sleep wasn't working like it did when I was a kid. I needed peace at night, but I just didn't know how to find it as I was maturing. I still couldn't sleep at home and the reason was still the same, my parent's drunken yelling and screaming. In the shadows of that Halloween evening, I walked till I was in a decent neighborhood and then watched all of the little kids in their purchased costumes. I didn't see a single white t-shirt or Zombie painted face. The parents in this neighborhood were respectable. You could tell by the pressed jeans, nice jackets, and tennis shoes that the dads and moms wore leading their little ones in purchased costumes about. Equally impressive, were the kind faces of older couples at doors holding big bowls of candy and their delight in making over each little kid that rang their bell. I kept walking and didn't speak to anyone. I wasn't dressed for the neighborhood and I didn't want anyone calling the police on me. I only had two pair of ragged jeans and I had worn them for three years.

I hadn't chosen a theme yet for the night. I decided it was impossible to window peep for the evening because there were too many people out and about celebrating and trick-or-treating. I headed for an apartment complex area where there were at least four hundred new apartments built in multiple high- rise buildings. I could sit on the first flight of stairs on any of them and watch the world go by with no problem. I just looked like a stranger, one of a mass of strangers living in and sharing ten buildings. I sat down on the outside stairs of the third building. Several couples wandered up and down with trash bags and grocery totes ignoring me. They probably assumed I lived somewhere in their building.

The sun had gone down. I watched a few adults wander down in costumes heading out to bars and parties. I needed something to count to pass the time. Sitting on the apartment complex first flight of stairs, I decided to count women wearing the color orange for the night. It was a simple choice. While waiting, I could sit and think about my future for awhile. The subject looming on my mind was what occupation I was going to choose after high school. My counselors were bugging me to make a choice so they could channel me to a job fair booth for seniors in the spring. They were determined they were going to set me up with a fast food or factory job. I just wanted them to leave me alone. I would think about an occupation after I got my final months of surviving in. It is hard to think about a job fair when you are trying to figure out when and where you are going to eat next.

In the back of my mind, I was considering working in a

car wash for a couple of months and then taking the cash and buying myself some decent clothes to wear to job interviews. No one but a car wash was going to hire me in my worn out clothes.

A woman pushed past me wearing an orange T-shirt with a pumpkin on the front. She was carrying a bag of kitchen trash down to the dumpster. She ignored me. She had a ponytail and was wearing a lot of eye makeup. I figured she had plans later. I eyed her feet in flip- flops. My woman would never wear cheap dollar flip flops from some low class discount chain. My woman would be kept in spikes and expensive tennis shoes. I was not going to be a flip flop man. The girl hadn't even bothered to remove the yellow sticker from the bottom of her ugly blue flippers. This was a nice apartment complex. In my mind, she was not putting her best foot forward. I counted her orange T-shirt and then ignored her. She was count one for the evening. I guessed it to be around seven. Cars were pulling in and getting out with grocery totes after work. There were a few parents descending from the apartments with a baby or toddler dressed for Halloween, probably headed for their grandmothers. Those babies had it made.

An older woman about forty made her way past me climbing up the stairs carrying a laptop case and a monstrous purse with a huge strap slung over her shoulder. She ignored me. I looked her over. She counted. She was carrying in her free hand a little clear cellophane wrapped bag containing Halloween candy. I could see some yellow and orange candy corn in the bag. Apparently, she was bringing it home from a possible office Halloween party. I did notice that she had great legs and wore black nylons. Her spikes were very plain, black, open toe, and hot looking. I was definitely a foot and leg man. She pleased me. Some-day, when I had a woman, I wanted her to be respectable and look like that, if she worked. My mother was about her age, but she looked like an old hag with raccoon eyes. Her feet hadn't seen a bottle of nail polish in ten years and didn't seem to give a damn how she looked. In retro think-ing, my stepfather looked equally as bad. The Candy Corn lady pleased me. She was number two of my six-count for the evening.

Everyone was ignoring me where I was sitting, so I just continued to sit and think. About fifteen minutes later, I watched a man jump out of his car in the parking area. He grabbed a real orange pumpkin from his car trunk and then sprinted up the stairs of the apartment complex next door. I grinned. I bet he had promised his kid a jack-o-lantern and was keeping his promise even though he was running late from work. I had asked my father once when I was young to help me carve a pumpkin given to me at school. I pictured in my elementary school mind a Hal-loween masterpiece. He was half drunk and mad because I asked. He took a screw driver raised his hand and with a force poked a hole in the little pumpkin and then stuck one of his cigarette stubs in the mouth. He took an ink pen and drew on two dots for eyes and then laughed. I didn't think it was funny because I wanted a jack- o- lantern like sat on the porches of the kids down the street. I never asked my father for anything after that. I was an unwanted kid that my father, mother, and grandmother ignored. I was good for a welfare check and food stamps to them, noth-ing more. I imagined the excited eyes of the kid upstairs who was going to have a father cut eyes and features into the pumpkin and a mother who was going to be all smiles and stick a candle in it. I would always be there for my kids, if I ever decided to have any. The pumpkin sprinting dad counted as number three.

I spotted an older woman in her sixties climbing the stairs of the seven floor apartment building next door. She was way too old to be climbing seven flights of stairs. I watched her spiral upwards. She carried a single grocery tote. She was bundled up and looked like she might be wearing two or three sets of clothing. "She must be a street person." I muttered and continued to watch her as she reached the third floor.

Someone whistling caught my attention. I looked around and spotted a man in an orange ball cap leaving a third floor apartment on the other side of me. As he descended the stairs, he was putting on an orange construction site vest. He hurried down the stairs, got in a pickup, and sped off. I would probably end up like him, alone and working on holidays. I didn't want to be alone. He was count number four.

I glanced at my watch which was Jackie's old one. She had given it to me when she got a new one as a graduation gift. It was about eight-thirty. Remembering the elderly street lady, I glanced up where the old woman was climbing. She was on the top walkway seven floors up. I watched her pass the last apartment door. Then I saw her step into a very narrow passageway. She was somehow heading for the roof. Did she sleep up there? I kept watching and it wasn't long till I saw her peep over the ledge on the roof and scan the night sky. She was smarter than me. Her nights were safe up there and she was sleeping in a good neighborhood. After all the foot traffic died down, I would make my way up there and see how she got on the roof. I had another seven months of high school to put in and I might need a reliable, safe place to sleep when the weather was good.

I turned my attention back to watching the apartment dwellers come and go. A plump woman in her thirties wearing a witches costume passed me sporting orange polished fingernails. I counted her as number five and wondered why she hadn't put on green nail polish which would have gone better with her costume. Glancing at her feet, I saw that she wore orange striped knee socks in black old lady lace up shoes. On a scale of one to ten in the feet department, she was a disaster. There were some women who had no taste. She had to be one of them. I wondered what kind of a party she was going to. She definitely wouldn't be a hit with any man if it was an adult one. She was not going to score. She was number five on my count for the evening.

For another thirty minutes or so, I watched adults come and go in work clothes and various costumes. In front of the apartment building next to where I sat, I saw an old dented up four door car pull in and a young dude maybe sixteen get out. He was wearing a black and white striped jail bird costume. He sprinted up two sets of stairs, knocked, and then escorted a young girl about fifteen down. She was wearing a maternity top and seemed to be in distress. I ran to help him. He was half way holding her up.

"Do you need some help?" I asked opening the passenger door of his beat up car to assist him. I recognized her from school. She was the pregnant girl that the jocks and cheerleaders made fun of.

"Thanks man. She is my sister and her baby is coming. She lives with our father on the second floor and he is gone for the evening. She called me for help. I was just getting ready to walk out the door and go to a Halloween party across town. Don't I know you?" he asked as I closed the door after he helped his sister in.

"I am Zeke from school. I work in the cafeteria at lunch. I have seen your sister almost every day. She drinks a lot of chocolate milk and eats a lot of onion rings with pickle relish on them."

"Pregnancy has done a thing to her taste buds. I am Bill and she is my step sister, Amy. We have different mothers. Thanks for your help. Would you be interested in riding over to the hospital with me and hanging out till this baby gets here. It looks like my Halloween party is a bust."

"I am headed up to the seventh floor of the building next door. My grandmother lives up there. She expects me to watch horror flicks with her for the evening. My Halloween night is a bust too." I stated lying. I didn't have my peeping count done. I still liked one orange item.

"Yell at me next week at school! I will tell you all about the birth of her little orange pumpkin." the boy in a jailbird costume stated getting in his car to drive away.

"I will do that!" I stated grinning and waving at the two of them bye. Maybe fate had brought them to me. I considered what he had said about the baby being an orange pumpkin delivery. I accepted it as the sixth of my count for the night. I waved and grinned as the pair sped off into the night. Glancing at my watch, I saw that it was about nine.

There didn't seem to be any further foot traffic for the moment. So, I started to spiral upwards to see if I could figure out how to get on the roof on the seventh floor. I had planned to sleep on the top of the fast food place after midnight. This was a step up in my book if the roof was easily accessible.

I was excited about the possibility of having a couple new friends. I didn't know that the girl would never return to school and the jailbird costumed boy would be dead by morning. They both ended up in a wreck just before they got to the hospital. He died. The baby was lost. The girl, I never saw again. Bill, the boy, had been drinking when his sister called asking him to come pick her up. My own parents were such sops that he looked sober next to them. I never considered that they would be the victims of alcohol. I would have treasured him as a friend. He slipped right thru my fingers. I have often wondered what good times I missed out on with him.

Once I reached the seventh floor, I leaned on the walkway railing and scanned the city. About a mile away, I could see a clump of trees in the old part of town and knew that my house and several others existed below the grove. My neighborhood was old and had hundreds of mature trees that no one could afford to trim or take down if dead. I watched from the seventh floor till I made sure all was quiet and no one was watching me. Then, I quickly stepped into the narrow passage that was at the end of the walkway. In the narrow passage, I spotted a metal fire ladder spanning the seventh floor wall to the roof. I began to climb. I wanted to experience the roof top and see if it was a possible sleeping place. When I reached the top, I peeped over making sure the elderly woman wasn't waiting to greet me with a knife or something to prevent my ass from climbing onto her turf. Surprisingly, she was sitting next to a heat exhaust pipe covered up with a thin quilt. I was sure she had stored the quilt up there on some previous night when she slept there.

"Welcome stranger," she said."Do you need to share my Gypsy's wagon tonight? The stars are bright and the spirit guides are speaking. Your name is Bump and your granny stands next to me whispering your name in my ear."

"Are you a friend of Granny Snoop?" I asked caught off guard as to what to say. I stepped onto the roof.

"I am friends with no one, but the spirits who come to speak are family and friends to many. I am Granny Snoop's mouthpiece for the evening. Come sit with me and we will delve into the world of the unknown."

"I don't believe much in the invisible or God. If God and Santa Claus were real they would have come to my aid years ago." I stated sitting down, pulling my knees up, and then circling my arms around my legs to sit and chat. She had my attention and definitely was an interesting character.

"I gather you are unhappy with your life and possibly need an experience with the supernatural to give you hope. Do you have a question or a mystery that you would like the otherworld to help you with?"

"Come to think of it, I do." I stated intending to trip her up with a question about Jodi Jones. "I have a friend that I used to hang out with that disappeared. I don't know whether she is alive or dead. What can you tell me about her?" I asked giving her no name or personal information.

"Her name is Josephine, not Jodi. According to Granny Snoop who stands here next to me, she is not dead. She just ran away. I see a card coming to you from her in May next year. I see money in it. Someday, you will find her. However, she will never return here. Her life here was bad, just like yours is in another. You wish to run, but your time hasn't come yet. I see a house fire as the turning point in your life. Tragedy will bring you a better life, but it will also bring you sorrow."

"I have been sleeping in a burnt out house for two or three years when needed. It hasn't brought me anything but an occasional asthma attack from the charred smell."

"By tomorrow night, you will be sleeping in a clean bed in a lock up facility for boys your age. It will not be a bad thing. You will have clean clothes, food, and start a journey to the life you want."

"Well, my gypsy friend, nothing ever changes for me. My life won't change till the day I graduate high school. What is your name? My name is Bump."

"I am Carmen the Flyer." She replied simply pulling a sandwich from her pocket and offering me half.

"Thanks, but I have already eaten." I said refusing the sandwich even though my gut was rolling with belly sounds. There was no telling when she had washed her hands and I was not about to catch anything from her. I did eat left over fast food, but I didn't share drinks or food otherwise if I could help it. "How did you get your name?"

"My parents were circus people. When I was young, I was a trapeze artist. As I grew older, I became the circus fortune teller because I had a gift for it."

"Is that why you are not afraid to climb up here and sleep?" I asked wrapping myself around an exhaust vent to warm myself like she was doing.

"I am a flyer. I have no fear of heights. I am psychic and have made my way to you. I have been waiting for you up here. I walk the Earth looking for souls like you who need me. I am the voice of those beyond the grave. I bring you messages from a Granny Snoop and a man I don't know. He is holding up a map of the state of California and pointing to you. Do you have family or friends there?"

"No, I replied not wanting to bring Jackie into it. I was trying to stay low key about her till I got my senior year in. The kids at school now snickered and teased me about being homosexual. I wondered how the funny dressed old Gypsy knew Granny Snoop. I quickly guessed she had to be a psychiatric patient of Granny Snoop.

"The man wishes to tell you that you will be in California next summer."

"That is interesting," I replied.

"I see your father cooking tonight." She added gazing into the sky.

"My father is a cook." I replied picturing my dad making meth in the garage before I left for the evening. I would just let her think he was a restaurant cook somewhere.

"Time is short, is there anything you wish to ask of the other world? I must fly away soon on silent wings. I was once a trapeze artist. I now fly on silent wings."

"I am a survivor. I will make it just fine. However, if I could ask a spirit to do anything for me, I would ask him to go to Jodi wherever she is and tell her that I am sorry about the dress and that I will always love her."

"It is an unselfish request. It is done. Granny Snoop is telling me to tell you to use your peeping talents in a new way. She says you should become a private detective and not peep unless you are paid for it. I hear her whispering that your days of counting to six are over. She says you should sleep days and be a detective at night and that will cure your problem."

"That is food for thought. I have never considered peeping as a vocation. Thanks, Carmen. I will tell the school's counselor that tomorrow. I need a vocation to put down for the senior's job fair."

"I see you receiving a fair size piece of money for graduation in May. Buy a camera with it and start a new life where your friend resides in California. The man with the California map says he is your spirit guide. His name is Spike."

"I have a spirit guide and his name is Spike?" I asked amused.

"Yes, he used to sit beneath your rod of clothes when you were three and four. You called him your imaginary friend named Spike. Your mother thought he was an imaginary dog."

"Damn, you are the real thing! I haven't thought about Spike in years. He would pretend he was a dog, let me pet him, and ride him like a horse. I wanted a dog bad back then."

"I am the real thing just like you will be the real thing in the detective business. Use your talents for good instead of a life of perverted peeping. You are past the need to count to six."

"You know about my peeping and the counting to six?" I gasped, a little taken back by the eerie encounter with a Circus trapeze artist slash Gypsy fortune teller.

She didn't answer because suddenly there was a huge boom that rocked the building top where we sat. We both almost jumped out of our skin. I made my way to the side of the rooftop ledge and looked into the distance. As near as I could tell, there was a fire in the neighborhood where I lived. The sky was lit up and you could see an orange ball that looked like a frightening Jack-o-Lantern laughing at me. I turned to make sure that Carmen was okay. She was standing on the ledge of the roof about twenty feet from me. Then in horror, I watched her jump."

I screamed and ran to the place where I saw her go over. In total shock, I then watched her flying like a bird across the night sky headed east.

"Oh shit, I have gone and lost it." I stated in disbelief. I walked over where the two of us sat warming ourselves. In utter fright, I saw looked down on myself asleep hugging an exhaust pipe that was blowing hot air. "I am either dreaming or having a nightmare." I muttered. Then frantically, I started to shake my body to wake it up."

The sun came up on November first before I was able to wake my sleeping body and slip back into it. I had an out of body experience that I will never forget. At seventeen I became a believer in the supernatural, Gypsy psychics, and spirit guides. Santa Claus, however, I still don't believe in, but I am keeping an open mind. I believe in what I see. I am a peeper.

CHAPTER THIRTEEN

LIFE TAKES A NEW DIRECTION

On waking after reentering my body, I jumped up and hurried to the side of the roof edge and looked toward my house. The smell of nasty, sweet, chemical smoke lingered in the air. My gut instinct told me that I had been kept on the apartment house roof top all night by Carmen and Spike to save my ass from burning to death in a meth explosion. I had no money for a bus or other transportation home. So, I was forced to speed walk home. It took about twenty minutes. Going to school was out of the question. I was already late for it anyway."

Finally reaching my street, I saw an array of forensic guys, ambulances, and police officers. When I neared the burnt rubble and saw that it was my house, I started running, screaming, and attempting to break thru the yellow police tape, but a policeman held me back.

"Let me go . . . my family!" I screamed bursting into tears.

"Are you the kid who lives here?" the policeman asked hanging on to my arm.

"Yes, I live here with my parents, grandmother and sister. I replied. Where are they?" I asked spanning a small crowd of on- lookers."

"Where were you all night?" the policeman asked not answering my question.

"I was visiting with a pregnant girl name Amy and a boy named Bill wearing a jail bird suit over in the Sky Walk Apartments. He drives an old dented four door. We go to the same school. I helped him get his pregnant sister Amy into his car so he could take her to the hospital. She was going into labor. I fell asleep on their balcony porch waiting for them to return. I just woke up." I replied half lying. There was no way that I was going to tell him I spoke with a spirit named Carmen and hallucinated for the night leaving my body.'

"I believe your story about the pregnant girl. I worked their car wreck last night."

"Wreck . . . they were in a wreck?"

"He was drinking and misjudged an off ramp. The boy didn't make it to the hospital. I am sorry."

All the blood drained from my face. Could this moment in time get any worse? "Bill is dead?"

"Yes, I am sorry. They hit a semi on the ramp. She lost the baby and he is dead."

"My family here, where are they?" I asked shook to my core. I had hoped Bill and I would become friends. I was really lonely.

"I am sure it is no secret to you, that your parents cook meth. They blew the garage and house up last night. Your mother is alive in the hospital. Your father, sister, and grandmother are dead. I am sorry. How old are you and do you have any family to call. You can't stay here."

"I have no one." I stated and then burst into tears and fell to my knees. I thought I hated my parents and wanted them to disappear until now. Somewhere in me was a tiny little shattered fragment piece of a heart that loved them in spite of everything. I just hadn't known it till now. "My mother, how serious is she?"

"Your mother has burns on her arms and hands. She was outside at the barbecue grill when the explosion took place destroying the garage and then the house. Your mother was blown toward the street and that saved her life. "

The policeman then put me in his cruiser and the rest is a blur. Just as Carmen predicted, I was taken to juvenile hall, gave a clean bed to sleep in, and was fed on a regular basis. There were charity boxes of used clothing there. The jeans and other items in the boxes were better than what I had on, so I chose two new outfits and threw the set I had on in the trash.

A social worker accompanied me to the grave side services for my father, sister, and grandmother. They were buried in pauper's row at the Catholic cemetery. They were cremated because there was no money for caskets and other items. They were charity burial cases. They went out like they lived, in self imposed poverty and shame. There was no one at the graveside services except me, the social worker, and a hospital chaplain who was donating his time to speak.

Standing listening to a stranger preach my family into Heaven speaking on the resurrection and the life, I felt so alone. I personally knew my family was in Hell. About the time the minister was into his ranting and carrying on, I felt a hand slip into mine squeezing my hand. I glanced to the side to see who it was. Thru my tears, I saw Jackie. She was dressed as a girl in black mourning clothes. She had flown in from California for the funeral. I threw myself into her arms and she held me while I cried. When I regained my composure and resumed my stance to hear the end of the chaplain's sermon, she leaned into me and whispered.

"I will always be there for you in the good times and bad, Bump. You were there for me."

I squeezed her hand and never wanted to let it go. I needed her and she was there for me. She was God's gift to me in my hour of despair, my bad time. The social worker wouldn't allow me to stay with her after the funeral. I was ushered back to Juvenile Hall. Jackie quickly wrote down my address on the back of her checkbook and stuck it in her black purse telling me she would come for me prom night and stay till I graduated high school. She told me not to ask anyone to the prom because that ticket was hers.

As the social worker was dragging me away, I yelled at Jackie. "Prom . . . Jackie, I want you in spikes and a killer dress."

She yelled back, "Good times and Bad!"

My mother did not attend the gravesides services because she was in the hospital with burns. I personally thought it was a cop out on her part. The social worker told me that the burns on her arms and hands were minor and that she was faking different symptoms to keep herself out of a jail cell. As I have said before, addicts and alcoholics are self centered. She should have been there for me if nothing else. She probably never gave me a second thought. I received no correspondence or phone calls from her while I was in Juvenile detention. I was on my own.

In my opinion my mother was better off in jail than on the streets hooking up with someone new to make meth with. She started my dad cooking when she met him promising him big bucks to buy sports cars and electronics. What he got was the loss of his daughter, the loss of his mother, a life of crime, addiction, alcoholism, and poverty. My mother was the dark force or devil in our family. She paved the road to Hell. I managed thru sheer determination to not dance in her flames.

After my stepfather, grandmother, and sister were laid to rest, my mother was charged and prosecuted for her part in the manufacture and distribution of meth. She was also charged with the deaths of my sister and grandmother who were drunk and passed out at the time. She made no effort to get them out of the house. I did not attend the trial except for a brief testimony on my part telling that my sister and Grandmother were drunk and passed out when I left the house to go trick-or-treating. The pregnant girl Amy was found and she told the police that I had indeed been at her apartment house and helped her into the car. I was moved from juvenile detention to a foster home for the remainder of my senior year. I testified against my mother. In my opinion, she was better off in prison where she couldn't ruin anyone else's life like she had mine and my sister's.

I found peace for the first time in my life. Juvenile detention was Heaven compared to the slum shack I had lived in. However, I couldn't sleep at night because I had never slept at night. When I did sleep, I dreamed of Carmen and she would tell me to hang in there and use my peeping for good. Social Services placed me as a foster child with a Jewish couple named Bill and Jenna Goldstein. I was one lucky seventeen year old senior boy. For the first time in my life, I found someone who took the time to love and care for me.

My foster mother, Jenna, baked cookies and never failed to provide me with clean clothes, a clean bed, and help with my homework which she personally inspected. She was everything I dreamed a mother could be. I copied down every recipe from her kitchen so I could pass them on to my children some day as coming from my mother. Jenna was sure that I was going to become a cook after high school because I lived and breathed in her kitchen. I loved everything about it including running the dishwasher and polishing her stainless steel refrigerator and stove. I was ashamed to tell her that her kitchen was the first I had ever been in that had food in it or pots and pans to cook in. My drunken parents sold everything they could get their hands on to make meth. That included the refrigerator, stove, dishes, pots and pans, anything and everything that was loose. I grew up eating with a plastic fork from the school cafeteria. Jenna's kitchen filled a hole in me that had never been filled. I always did the dishes and anything else she asked so she wouldn't kick me out. I feared returning to the wrong side of town and its hells. I didn't understand that there were people like her that liked kids and took them in to give them a chance, not kick them out.

Jenna's recipes are in my kitchen today and her and my foster dad's photos are on my nightstand along with one of Jodi, Jackie, and Granny Snoop. I snuck in Granny Snoop's house after she died and took a photo of her and one of Jodi. I didn't take anything else. I had to have a picture, a piece of them. I stored the two photos in my school locker till I was out of high school along with my birth certificate. Even though I loved my foster parents, I just wasn't sure of who to trust. I kept my treasures at school in my locker a secret. The photos of the women in my life were my greatest treasures. My alcoholic parents warped me in the trust department. Today, I would trust Bill and Jenna Goldstein with anything I have. It took time to turn the loose screw in my head.

Jenna, my foster mother, became to me the pattern for respectability. I often ask myself if she will approve of what I am doing. I measure my life by her. I bought a recipe box just like hers when I got my first apartment. I wanted my kitchen to be filled with love and food just like hers. She could bake one mean sugar cookie that was the size of a saucer. She never fails to make me a tin of them when she comes to visit. My foster dad is retired and flies out when I am on a big case and need a second pair of eyes. I have hooked him on being a detective and he is now, my best friend.

My seven months with my foster parents was peaceful and wonderful. I had never been inside of a synagogue, art museum, or theatre. They introduced me to worlds that I never knew existed including, fine restaurants, bookstores, and fine men's wear stores. They taught me to golf, play tennis, and fish. My foster dad took me to ball games and car races. When I left their home, I was dressed like a respectable man my age and had been given a crash course in social graces. At the end of my senior year, the girls actually saw me as a hunk which was new for me. I had nice clothes and looked like every other respectable up-per class kid at school. However, I never dated any of the girls. I remembered how they treated me when I was poor and owned two pair of three year old tattered jeans. I also remembered how the kids treated Jackie because she was different and Amy the pregnant girl. I am loyal to those who are loyal to me. I will always make an attempt to be there in the bad times for those I love.

A week before graduation, a card made its way to me, having been forwarded a couple of times thru the social services offices. When I saw who it was from, I cried. There was no return address, but inside was a graduation card and a money order made out to me for one hundred dollars. It was from Jodi. She wrote simply on the inside:

"I WISH you had been a little older when I left. I would have taken you with me. I checked on line and saw that you are in the graduating class. I am proud of you for hanging in there. I want you to take this money and pur-chase yourself a camera. I never plan on returning. Create a good life for yourself and don't tell anyone that you have heard from me. Love, Jodi.

P.S. You were right about the dress and the fact that I should have went to prom with you. I can now see what a fool I was. Love, Jodi."

Checking out the envelope, I saw that it was stamped by the post office of Jackson, Florida. I would find her some-day. She was as much a part of me as Jackie was. I took her card and stored it in my school locker with my other pho-tos, birth certificate, and a print out from the internet of a trapeze artist that had died in the 1950's named Carmen. Having a computer and internet at my foster home helped me step forward into my new life and the information age. I was a quick learner and my father a patient teacher. I was clueless about most everything having never had anything for the first seventeen years of my life.

Graduation arrived. Jackie did fly back to go to the prom with me and stayed till I graduated. I flew back to California with her and my foster parents paid for my ticket and gave me five thousand dollars to start over there. For prom, Jackie wore a killer pair of purple open toed spikes and a rented stewardess dress. She also rented the pilot's costume for me. My mother Jenna cried when we left for the prom after taking multiple photos of us. She kissed us both and told us to have the best night of our life. My foster father tossed me the keys to his vintage baby blue mustang. They were okay with Jackie and me. What more could a foot man ask for. I found family in my darkest hour. My foster father accepted Jackie just as he did me. Jenna and Abraham Goldstein are my parents. I found them late in life. I was almost a man when they took me in and loved what was left of the child in me. When my detective agency prospered and I had money in my pocket for special things, I went to court and had my legal last name changed to Goldstein. I am loyal to those who love me.

My birth mother, Trudy, spent fifteen years in prison. I never went to see her during that time. She ignored me when I was a child and let me go hungry day after day. I felt I owed her nothing. In my mind, she would return to drugs and alcohol when she got out of prison. She did and is now in prison for life. She robbed a convenience store and killed the clerk three months after she was out for a bottle of Vodka and thirteen dollars. I have no intentions of keeping in touch with her. Granny Snoop was right. You have to make choices. I have chosen not to walk in hell with my birth mother, but in Heaven with Jenna. Jenna Goldstein has been my mother for fifteen or so good years.

My advice to kids in bad situations is to take your talents, whatever they are, and create a good life for yourself when your time comes. Also, don't be afraid of the social worker who calls. She could be the one person who really cares about you and is your ticket out. My foster parents were the best thing that ever happened to me.

I am still a foot man and own a detective agency called "ZEEK'S FEET". It is named after the women in my life who all have beautiful feet; Jodi, Jackie, Jenna, Carmen, and Granny Snoop.

Carmen if you and Spike are out there listening; thanks for pointing me in the right direction.

Granny Snoop, I now understand the pain of making good choices. I have had to abandon my mother just as you did your son to walk in respect and the light. Someday, I will find Jodi and point her toward the light of your choices.

THE END

Also by Jo Hammers

Tattootie

The Joel Manuscript

Zook's Place

Black Lightning Series

Seven Secret Wives, Book 1

Naomi's Dream, Book 2

www.ingramcontent.com/pod-product-compliance
Lightning Source LLC
Chambersburg PA
CBHW051239170626
46809CB00004B/1397